"About last night, Hannah," Alex said

"I'd give anything to be able to undo it." He touched her face. "I couldn't work out what you were trying to get at. Want to tell me now?"

"I think . . ." she whispered, then found she couldn't tell him any more than she could last night. "I think I still sometimes don't believe that this—you and me—is real. . . ."

"Then I'll have to show you," he said very quietly. "Before that, though, I'll have to tell you that I love you, Hannah, and you must never doubt it."

"You don't have to say that."

"Why not? It's true."

Hannah hid her face in his shoulder and thought, yes, it's true—in a way, I know that, but is it the same kind of love you . . . you had with her?

LINDSAY ARMSTRONG married an accountant from New Zealand and settled down—if you can call it that—in Australia. A coast-to-coast camping trip later, they moved to a six-hundred-acre mixed-grain property, which they eventually abandoned to the mice and leeches and black flies. Then, after a winning career at the track with an untried trotter, purchased "mainly because he had blue eyes," they opted for a more conventional family life with their five children in Brisbane, where Lindsay now writes.

Books by Lindsay Armstrong

HARLEQUIN ROMANCE
2443—SPITFIRE
2497—MY DEAR INNOCENT
2582—PERHAPS LOVE
2653—DON'T CALL IT LOVE

HARLEQUIN PRESENTS
559—MELT A FROZEN HEART
607—ENTER MY JUNGLE
806—SAVED FROM SIN
871—FINDING OUT
887—LOVE ME NOT

Some Say Love

Lindsay Armstrong

Harlequin Books

TORONTO • NEW YORK • LONDON
AMSTERDAM • PARIS • SYDNEY • HAMBURG
STOCKHOLM • ATHENS • TOKYO • MILAN

Original hardcover edition published in 1986
by Mills & Boon Limited

ISBN 0-373-02785-0

Harlequin Romance first edition September 1986

HANNAH Hawthorn stared upwards apprehensively and kept her finger on the button marked seven. But, as had happened to her several times in the last few minutes, the number seven on the board above the doors glowed and the lift stopped smoothly—only to commence a descent without the doors opening. What was worse, however, was that the mechanism adopted the same playful attitude at the second floor. The lift stopped coyly and then, without the doors opening, shot upwards to stop at the seventh floor again, only this time the doors did open. As Hannah was in the act of sliding thankfully out, however, a tall, male form dashed in, all but knocking her over.

'Oh no!' she gasped, as the doors started to close. 'Look—now look what you've done!' she cried, going white with fright as she realised the skirt of her dress was caught in the closed doors.

'I've done?' the man said. 'Oh, your dress. Hang on, there's no need . . .' He stopped as Hannah grappled furiously with the skirt of her dress and it came free with an ominous ripping sound.

'There was no need to do that,' he said mildly as he surveyed the skirt, now torn from waist to hem more from Hannah's frantic handling than anything else.

'Yes there was,' she panted. 'You don't understand, this lift is playing up! It'll start to go down now and with my dress caught in the doors I could have . . . been . . . anything,' she said palely as she visualised being strangled by her own dress. 'I mean . . .' She slumped to her knees as much from an unparalleled sensation of numbness as from the fact that the lift had indeed started to go down only to stop abruptly. She swallowed and put a hand to her mouth. 'I feel sick,' she muttered.

'I'd try not to think about that,' her companion said with a tinge of amusement and knelt down beside her.

She looked up into a pair of dark, sleepy eyes beneath thick, dark hair sprinkled with grey and set in a strong, tanned face.

'Which floor are we at now?' she asked tremulously.

He glanced up briefly. 'I'd say between the third and the fourth since both numbers are blinking and we seem to be stationary.'

'I hate lifts!' Hannah exclaimed passionately. 'I always have. I always knew I was going to get stuck in one . . .'

The man raised his eyebrows quizzically but said soothingly, 'If one was to go into the statistics of it, I'm sure you'd find that lift travel is far safer than most other forms of transport.'

'You might be right but give me a plane or a horse anytime!' she said fervently and turned on him. 'And I don't see how you can bother with statistics at a time like this, because we're just as liable to end up as statistics ourselves! For all we know the cables might be frayed—that could be why it's acting so strangely. Quite possibly we're about to be tipped down the shaft to . . . crash!'

'Hey,' he said quietly, and sat down on the floor pulling her into his lap as if she was a child, 'believe me, that's highly unlikely so there's no need to get into a sweat . . .'

'But I am,' she interrupted. 'I really am. You see I've been stuck in this stupid lift for ages so . . .'

'We are not going to crash.' He over-rode her firmly. 'It's simply a question of the electronics playing up and in no time at all someone will realise it because I've pressed the alarm button. What did you say your name was?'

'Hannah. At least I didn't——'

'Hannah,' he said musingly. 'I like that. It has a good, solid ring to it.'

She cast him a bitter look. 'If you only knew what an enormous cross being called Hannah Rose——' She stopped abruptly as he moved his hand over her hair in much the same fashion her father used to. She bit her lip and said in a small voice, 'I'm sorry, I'm being quite ridiculous, aren't I? It's just that I got such a fright.'

'I know,' he said. 'But that's understandable if lifts give you claustrophobia. I'm sure you're not the only person to suffer from it, either.'

'I suppose that's what it is,' she said in some surprise. 'A form of claustrophobia. I don't seem to get it about anything else though. Isn't that strange!' She relaxed somewhat and thought about it and, as a sort of natural projection from those thoughts, found herself marvelling at how safe she felt suddenly, sitting in this man's lap with his arm round her . . .

She jerked upright and would have scrambled off his lap if he'd let her then, but instead, his lips twitched as he surveyed her suddenly red face, and those sleepy eyes came alive with laughter. 'What is it now?' he murmured.

Hannah had the acute feeling that he knew exactly what it was; that he had read her thoughts as if they'd been printed on her face and when she started to speak and stopped confusedly, he confirmed it by saying, 'How old are you, Hannah?'

'Eighteen. What's that got to do with it?' she asked in some exasperation.

He shrugged. 'It's just that I'm old enough to be your father.'

That doesn't mean ... anything,' she said doubtfully.

'Well, it does,' he replied. 'It doesn't mean I'm altogether past it, as you so rightly surmise.' His eyes teased her wickedly. 'It does mean, however, when one gets to my age, one has generally learnt a bit of self-control. So if you're worried that I'm going to leap on you, you shouldn't be. Relax, kid,' he added kindly and ruffled her hair.

Hannah subsided. But she felt as if she'd been effectively reduced to the age of twelve and experienced a curious pang of irritation. She looked down at her dress and fingering the ripped skirt, sighed unconsciously.

'Why the sigh, Hannah?' he queried. 'We will get out of here, I promise you.'

'Oh, it wasn't that,' she said and clutched his hand as the lift started to move. 'I was thinking of my dress. I was very fond of it—it was my best dress.' She spoke hastily to take her mind off what the lift was doing—it had stopped again, but the doors remained firmly closed. 'I was wearing it to, well, impress the person I was on my way to see before this stupid lift began to act up. I'll have to go home now and,' she sighed again, 'gather up my courage once more,' she finished with a wry little smile.

'Perhaps you could explain what happened?'

Hannah thought for a bit. Then she said, 'It was going to be awkward enough, in a way, as it was—no, he's bound to think I'm some kind of a freak. I mean, I have this unfortunate habit of getting myself into all sorts of scrapes as it is. To *arrive* all tattered and torn—no.'

'Is this a business call you're ... you were attempting to make?' her companion enquired, his lips quirking with amusement.

'Not *exactly*,' Hannah replied. 'It's a personal thing too. The problem is, he's a very busy man. I mean I've rung several times but they won't even pass my name on—at least I don't think they could have because—but anyway, that's why I decided to take the bull by the horns today, in a manner of speaking.' She grimaced ruefully.

'I get those days too. The kind when you feel you should have stayed in bed.'

'Do you?' she asked, a little eagerly.

He laughed. 'Don't we all. But about your dress, perhaps it could be mended?' He looked down at her skirt. 'I'm no expert though, I have to confess,' he added.

'Well,' Hannah said doubtfully, 'I don't think so without it showing. Never mind though, as my father used to say—the Lord shall provide—I'll just have to trust in that. W-what's happening now?' she said, as she held his hand tighter.

'I think we're about to be rescued,' the man said slowly, and Hannah looked at him to see that he was studying her curiously. 'What is it?' she asked.

'I—don't know,' he replied with a faint frown. He shook his head and shrugged. Then he eased his hand out of hers to dig it into his pocket and pull out two fifty dollar bills. 'Consider me in the nature of Providence, Hannah,' he said with a grin, and put the money into her hand.

Hannah stared at it and then up at him with a stricken look in her eyes. 'I couldn't!' she said agitatedly. 'I didn't mean ... did you think ... oh, heavens!' she muttered, deeply embarrassed and colouring brightly. 'No ...'

'Yes,' he contradicted her firmly. 'You see I'd hate to think of you without a pretty dress to give you confidence for your mysterious encounter ... in fact, just without a pretty dress.' The lift doors slid open but the man took no notice. Instead, with a devilish, wicked glint in his eyes, he kissed Hannah gently on the lips and went on, 'Because, while I was loath to admit it just now, Hannah, I doubt if any man alive could feel fatherly towards you, you're far too lovely for that.'

Hannah stared up at him, shaken and strangely breathless. Then she turned her head and to her horror, realised that not only a white-overalled mechanic but a group of about ten other people, were staring into the lift with varying expressions of surprise and amusement on their faces.

'Oh!' she whispered, and tried to give the money back.

It was not accepted. Instead she was lifted to her feet, patted on the head once more ... and the man was gone with a murmured, 'Sorry to dash off like this but I'm late as it is ...'

'But ...' Hannah stammered, 'I can't accept this.' She held the money up at the same time as the foyer doors closed behind her recent companion. Then her eyes focused on the deeply interested audience confronting her, and she looked down at her torn skirt and up again to see a few knowing grins and winking eyes. 'It isn't ... it's not what you think,' she stammered. 'It ... oh, God!' And she too was hurrying towards the foyer doors thinking, just let me get out of here. How *could* he ...

                    *   *   *

An hour or so later, Hannah was back at the Rectory and recounting her experience to Mrs Clayton, the minister's wife, who was listening with wide-eyed interest. The Reverend Clayton had been a friend of Hannah's father, the Reverend Hawthorn, which was why Hannah was availing herself of a long-standing invitation to stay with the Claytons who ministered to the Anglican souls of Surfer's Paradise.

'Well,' Mrs Clayton said, as Hannah finished speaking. 'I don't see what the problem is. The Lord does work in mysterious ways, Hannah, as Mr Clayton continually points out to me,' she added a shade ruefully.

'I know that,' Hannah said.

'Then what's the problem?' Mrs Clayton enquired and added practically, 'You could pay it back in instalments when you get a job.'

'But I don't know his name!'

'Didn't you think to ask?'

'No,' Hannah said somewhat darkly.

'My dear,' Mrs Clayton studied her for a moment before going on, 'from what you've told me, he behaved like a perfect gentleman towards you.'

'Yes,' Hannah said slowly and thought of a pair of dark, sleepy eyes that were often not sleepy at all. 'I mean, yes, he did,' she said confusedly. 'But afterwards he left me with a hundred dollars in my hand and—well, it looked . . . it looked very strange indeed.'

'What did?' the minister asked, coming in unexpectedly. 'You're home, Hannah! Did you get to see him?'

'No,' Hannah said desolately. 'I got stuck in a lift, I tore my best dress and I met a man who gave me some money to buy a new dress, and if you must know, I've never been so totally humiliated in all my life.' She raised her grey eyes suddenly. 'He kissed me, in front of everyone and it looked as if we'd . . . made love in the lift!' She looked down again and sniffed tearfully.

The Reverend Clayton and his wife looked at each other over the top of Hannah's head until Mrs Clayton said, 'Hannah, dear, don't upset yourself. If it was only a kiss—well, he might have had a strange sense of humour. At least he didn't kiss you—I mean, it would have been worse if there'd been no one to see, in a way. And so far as the hundred dollars goes, we can give it to the church fund if you really don't want to accept it, and Ted and I would be only too happy to help you out in the matter of a new dress. Wouldn't we, Ted?' She glanced at her husband who nodded energetically although with a comical look of bewilderment.

'No.' Hannah raised her hot, tear-streaked face suddenly. 'Thank you very much,' she said quietly but firmly. 'You're both so sweet, but I guess in a sense I'm almost as needy as the church fund at the moment, so I *will* use his money.' She tilted her chin defiantly and then smiled through her tears and stood up. 'By the way, I'm cooking dinner tonight!'

'My dear, you're our guest,' Mrs Clayton protested. But Ted Clayton put a hand over hers and said, 'You go ahead, Hannah. I've always found it helps . . .'

'You've never cooked dinner in your life, Ted,' Mrs Clayton said wryly, as Hannah left the room.

'Only because you won't let me loose in your kitchen.' Ted Clayton smiled warmly at his wife. 'I *meant*, it helps to work off one's grievances . . . Look, before I expire of curiosity, will you please tell me what happened this afternoon?'

'Oh dear,' his wife replied with a chuckle, 'I'll try, but I'm a little confused myself . . .'

Hannah looked at herself in the mirror of the small dressing-room and thought, this is *it*!

She turned sideways, admiring the way the azalea pink dress fell and how it complemented her pale, smooth skin, grey eyes and thick cap of dark, shining hair. The material was some synthetic that looked like silk, but would probably be a whole lot easier to care for and the style was the last word in quiet sophistication—a pleated bodice with a cravat neck, elbow length sleeves gathered into a narrow cuff, and a demurely gathered skirt.

'Much smarter than my other one,' she murmured and then grimaced. 'Probably dearer too,' she added, as she twisted round awkwardly to find the price tag.

Oh well, she thought as she let the tag fall, it is the kind of dress I could wear anywhere and by a stroke of luck I've got a pair of shoes to go with it. And when one looks around, ninety-nine dollars just doesn't go anywhere these days, not in Surfer's Paradise anyway! And it is important to make a good first impression.

Then she laughed quietly at the expression on her face and said to her reflection the mirror, 'Admit it, Hannah, so long as you have one hundred dollars resting in your purse, there's no way you could resist this dress despite the manner in which you acquired the money!'

Her face grew thoughtful though, as from long habit she pondered her secret and almost sinful craving for beautiful clothes, a craving that until now, had never had a chance to be fulfilled to any great extent. Perhaps I should discipline myself, she mused. After all, didn't Dad always say you should never judge a person by their clothes? Then again, he had such a presence, no one ever gave his clothes another look. And if it's an investment in my future . . .

She fingered the tie-ends of the cravat and suddenly found herself thinking of something quite different. Of a pair of dark eyes and whether they would approve of her in this dress. Her face grew hot again as she thought of the events of the previous day. Then a certain wilful light entered her eyes as she remembered the stark agony of being left clutching a hundred dollars in one hand and her torn skirt in the other . . .

'I will take it,' she muttered and took the dress off carefully. She reached for her denim skirt and blouse and jumped as the sales-lady came into the booth.

'What's that, pet? Didn't you like it?'

'I loved it and I'll take it,' Hannah said, recovering herself.

'I thought you might,' the saleslady said. 'It's you, a young style, but chic and you have the figure for it, really slender, but nicely curved in all the right places, Classy—like the dress.'

Hannah paused in the act of buttoning up her blouse. 'Do you really think so?'

'I know so,' the saleslady said with a grin and picked up Hannah's wrist. 'You can see it in the ankle and the wrists and the waist and the bust and those lovely long legs. Oh, I can tell class a mile off. Is it for a special occasion?'

'Hopefully, many special occasions,' Hannah said wryly.

Now I simply will not allow myself to be cowardly about this, Hannah thought, as she stood that afternoon in the same foyer that had seen her so humiliated only the day before.

'I shall just hope to God nobody recognises me,' she muttered to herself, 'and I *will* take the lift to the seventh floor. On the law of averages alone, I must be safe, surely.'

All the same, she sent up a little prayer for some divine assistance to the law of averages as she entered the lift, and couldn't help herself from shivering slightly. The lift, however, behaved perfectly and she stepped out on the seventh floor and looked around and perceived her quarry. Or rather, she saw the outward manifestation of it in the form of a sign painted on a door which said simply—ALEX CAMERON—BLOODSTOCK AND REAL ESTATE.

Hannah drew a deep breath and went through the doorway.

'Can I help you?' a rather distracted looking receptionist asked her, as Hannah's shoes sank into carpet that was inches deep.

Hannah glanced around at the beautifully panelled, elegantly decorated area and then back to the receptionist who was just as decorative, for all her air of strain. 'I'd like to see Mr Cameron, please,' she said nervously. 'My name is . . .'

'I'm so sorry,' the receptionist interrupted very firmly, 'but unless you have an appointment, that's impossible.' She tapped the counter with her pen and Hannah got the clearest impression that she was barely suppressing a flurry of impatience as she then began to riffle through a stack of papers.

Hannah lifted her chin slightly. 'So you keep telling me,' she said. 'I mean on the phone—that he's impossibly busy. And you keep telling me to ring back in a few days but it's been weeks now! Surely he can't be that busy and I know he'll understand once he gets to see me.'

The receptionist cast her large blue eyes heaven-wards. 'If you only knew,' she muttered and looked as if she was counting to ten beneath her breath. If she was, it seemed to help her regain her composure because she said then with a charming smile, 'I'm afraid he is that busy. He has a big yearling sale coming up in a few days and our routine has been unexpectedly disrupted, unfortunately. Which is why he's left strict instructions that anything of a personal nature . . .'

'It's not . . . I mean it is something personal, but— not really, if you know what I mean,' Hannah interrupted. 'What I mean is, *I've* never met him . . .' She trailed off helplessly.

'Then much better to leave it until after the . . . unless you've come from the employment agency?' the receptionist asked with a sudden, unmistakable gleam of hope in her eyes.

'Em . . . no . . .' Hannah stopped as an inner door opened, and froze as a tall man came out, leafing through a sheaf of papers he had in his hand and for a moment oblivious to her presence as he said, 'Sylvia, I need the rest of this stuff urgently. Have you finished it . . . hell!' he uttered, as he lifted his head and his gaze rested on the pile of papers the girl had been shuffling a few minutes earlier, and then passed on to Hannah.

'Not yet, Mr Cameron,' Sylvia replied in some agitation and added, 'This lady insists on seeing you, by the way. I've told her . . .' She shrugged.

Hannah came out of her trance and said disbeliev-ingly, 'You!' as she once again found herself staring into a pair of sleepy dark eyes.

'Why, Hannah,' Alex Cameron replied in amused surprise, 'we meet again.'

Hannah shut her mouth with a click and blushed. 'I don't understand,' she said feebly. 'You can't be Alex Cameron. At least, not the one I expected. Do you have a father? I mean . . .' She stopped uncertainly.

'I did. His name was Brian. By the way,' he looked her over appreciatively, 'if that's the new dress, I like it very much.'

Hannah closed her eyes in silent mortification. How *could* this happen to me? she thought.

Her eyes flew open as the girl Sylvia murmured then, 'I'm sorry, I didn't realise you knew the . . . uh . . . lady, Mr Cameron. *She* said . . .'

'I . . .' Hannah interrupted hurriedly.

Alex Cameron, in turn, interrupted her, 'You wanted to see me, Hannah? About yesterday?'

'Oh no,' Hannah said with some irony. 'I . . . well, according to my father,' she added helplessly, 'you were a good friend of his and he asked to be remembered to you just before he died. He said, when you meet up with Alex Cameron, Hannah, remind him of the horses we broke in on the Barcoo . . .'

A sudden stillness came over Alex Cameron and his eyes were piercingly intent as they probed Hannah's face. Then he said very quietly, 'Of course. I knew there was something about you, but I couldn't put my finger on it. Now, I can't imagine why not—you're so like him you couldn't be anyone but . . . Hannah Hawthorn?'

'Yes,' Hannah said tremulously and wiped away a tear. 'I'm sorry. I thought I'd got over that. Anyway,' she tried to smile, 'he spoke of you sometimes and he was always sure I'd meet you one day, but I always seemed to miss you for some reason or another. I think I was away at school the last time he saw you . . .'

'And I was overseas when he died,' Alex said with a

frown. 'I didn't even hear about it until a month or so ago. I thought it was too late to do anything—which just goes to show I didn't think very well at all.'

'Oh,' Hannah said awkwardly, 'you were right really.' She pressed her palms together. 'I won't take up any more of your time . . .'

'Wait, Hannah,' he said peremptorily as she half turned towards the door. 'I'll come with you.' He put the sheaf of papers down on Sylvia's counter. 'It's impossible to talk here without being interrupted. If anyone needs me I'll be back in an hour or so,' he said to the open-mouthed Sylvia and added with a grin, 'Don't worry, we'll get through somehow—the Lord provides!'

'But where . . . what . . .?' Hannah said confusedly.

'Somewhere quiet. Did you come up by lift?' he asked amusedly.

'I . . . yes,' she said and added uncertainly, 'but . . .'

He shepherded her through the doorway and grinned at her. 'That was brave of you. I just thought we could go somewhere and catch up on old times. It seems I have a lot of catching up to do. Your father was . . . the best friend I ever had.'

Hannah hesitated no longer.

'That's quite a tale, the story of your life, Hannah,' Alex Cameron said to her some time later. 'Did you never think it was a strange life for a girl, travelling round the outback with your father?'

Hannah said frankly, 'Oh no! The only regrets I had were those times I was forced to spend away from him and the fact that I'd been born a girl and not a son for him. Perhaps then I could have gone on and become a priest too, like he was, and been attached to the Inland Mission although,' she shrugged, 'I don't think . . . I mean, I often doubt that I have a true vocation.'

'Why's that?' he asked with a slight smile.

'For one thing I don't seem to have inherited his complete indifference to things material. It was easier when he was around but he's only been gone for three months and this very morning I allowed myself to be seduced into paying ninety-nine dollars for a dress! Oh!' she added and turned pink as he burst out laughing, and she hoped desperately that the dim, cool interior of the little bistro they were in camouflaged her hot cheeks.

Then she found she had to smile, although reluctantly, and she said ruefully, 'I *knew* I shouldn't have used that money. If I'd known I was going to run into you again I wouldn't have, believe me, because you embarrassed me dreadfully yesterday,' she added, with a spurt of resentment.

'I'm sorry about that,' he said with a grin. 'I'm afraid I couldn't resist it. However, now you know who I am, I hope I may have redeemed myself?' He looked at her quizzically.

She hesitated then said gruffly, 'Of course. Any friend of my father's is . . .'

'Automatically above reproach?' he supplied for her a little drily. 'Tell me about school,' he went on before she had a chance to answer. 'You may not realise it, but whenever you mention it, you sound rather disparaging.'

Hannah pulled a face. 'Considering how I hated it for the most part, I'm not surprised,' she said truthfully. 'If I'd been allowed to have my way I'd never have gone. I didn't see the least need for it. Between the School of the Air and what my father taught me, I was in fact a lot better educated than quite a few of the girls who'd been there all their lives.'

'I'm surprised you allowed yourself to be sent then,' he said gravely, but with a suspicion of a quirk tugging at his lips.

Hannah sighed. 'Unfortunately several well-meaning ladies got to my father and persuaded him that since I'd been without a mother for so long and since the diocese was very grateful to him for all he'd done for them—he was a lot more than just a minister to them, he was a doctor and nurse and vet and lawyer and counsellor . . . I don't have to tell you what it's like in those outback parishes probably; anyway they hit upon a plan whereby they could repay him for all he'd done. Which was to send me to an exclusive boarding school for the last eighteen months of my schooling. They put it to him that I'd learn to be a lady and make friends and so on and so on. He fell for it,' she said wistfully.

'Poor Hannah,' Alex Cameron sympathised. 'Was it very bad learning to be a lady? At least their conception of one?'

'Well,' she temporised, then said ruefully, 'actually a lot of it was my fault. Not only because I didn't want to go, but also because . . . well, it's a bit unnerving to be suddenly put into such a different environment. When I get . . . nervous, I get sort of prickly and on the defensive. Do you know what I mean?'

His eyes softened and he nodded. 'Go on.'

'Then, of course, there was the fact that I was used to a much freer kind of education, which I thought was a lot better actually. When I told them my father was an Oxford graduate and probably better qualified to teach me than they were, though, they didn't really appreciate it although they had to swallow their pride when I won the History prize in my first term.'

He laughed silently. 'They must have wondered what had hit them. Didn't you make any friends?'

'Yes, I did. But it wasn't easy,' she confessed. 'What with being on the defensive—an awful sin, I know, but something I find hard to fight—and telling them what I thought of their systems and their utter materialism and being quite a snob in reverse, I attracted a nickname that someone devised from my unfortunate initials.' She stopped and glanced at him, to see a sudden gleam in his eyes.

'Hannah Rose Hawthorn,' he murmured. 'H.R. . . . Her Royal Highness?' he hazarded. 'You poor kid,' he added as she nodded wryly.

'But it's Rosemary, after my mother.'

'Do you remember your mother, Hannah? I only met her once—before you were born.'

'Only vaguely because I wasn't quite six when she died. Do you know, my father never really got over her death, I think. Not that he went about miserable and mourning all the time. But sometimes he looked . . . inexpressibly lonely and I just knew it was for her. When he died, although he was so worried about me, he'd been without her for so long . . . well,' she said huskily, 'I like to think of them reunited somewhere at last. I had him for eighteen years . . .'

'He was a great man, your father,' Alex said a few minutes later, when she'd recovered her composure. 'Did he ever tell you what he did for me?'

'No. Just that you were friends. Good friends.'

'We weren't when we first met because I was a callow youth at the time, hell-bent on a course of destruction that led me to the Barcaldine watch-house on several occasions, and a few others round the west . . . He was sent to talk to me once—I think I was about fifteen and I'd been pretty literally dragged up, one of ten kids with an alcoholic father, not that I'm making excuses, but anyway—he was sent to talk some sense into me. Which I thought was a big laugh being at that age and so-minded anyway. You know, the idea of a Pommie priest who talked like no one I'd ever heard before, trying to tell me how to run my life.' He shrugged expressively. 'Anyway, not too long after that particular episode, I did something else, but to his private property, that was crude and when I look back now, unbelievable. At the time I thought there was no way he could *prove* I'd done it although I'd taken care to make sure he knew it. He didn't even try to prove it. He just cornered me one day in a dusty paddock with not a soul in sight, and beat the living daylights out of me. Much to my considerable surprise! Then he cleaned me up and offered to teach me all he knew about horses. He knew more about them than I'd believed possible. I mean about breeding and so on. Which,' he said slowly, 'is why I've achieved what I have today. I stayed with him for three years and I didn't only learn about horses. I learnt to *want* to learn and grow in every direction. He made me see beyond my own tough, incredibly narrow, little world.'

'I think he was very fond of you,' Hannah said. Then she grimaced. 'That doesn't say it very well. I had no idea how it happened. I just thought you were great friends. He often used to say you stimulated him.'

Alex Cameron looked down at the half finished drink in front of him. Then he said slowly, 'I often think that was my greatest achievement. Not so much the success I made of my life, thanks to him, but the fact that we became equals and real friends. And it was a friendship that endured despite the fact that we only saw each other perhaps half a dozen times over the last ...' He looked up suddenly. 'How old are you? Eighteen you said? Eighteen years then.'

Hannah glowed with pleasure. 'I very nearly went

away without telling you who I was this afternoon.
I'm glad I didn't now . . .' She tensed slightly as she
saw the frown of curiosity that came to his eyes.

'Did you come all the way down here to tell me
that? Or are you living down here now?'

'I . . . I'm staying with friends of my father's,' she
said uncomfortably.

'For how long?'

'I'm not sure. Until I go back,' she added and
winced.

'Back where?' His dark eyes narrowed.

'Oh, I'm not quite sure about that either,' she said
vaguely.

'Do you have a job?'

'N-no. Not yet. But I have the offer of plenty,' she
said and thought, that's true anyway.

'What kind of jobs?'

'Mainly governessing.'

He studied her thoughtfully. 'Is that what you
want? To be a governess to someone else's children?'

Hannah stared at her hands and wondered why she
found it so difficult to lie. Of course it should always
be difficult, she thought wryly. Normally she found it
was not one of the great problems of her young life,
but it seemed strangely hard to tell this man she'd
sought him out on her father's recommendation. Not
that she'd ever had cause to doubt her father's
wisdom, but she couldn't help feeling Alex Cameron
was a strange choice of person to help her find her
feet, although one thing her father had said was now
clarified . . .

'. . . You don't want to bury yourself in these back
blocks, Hannah,' those dry lips had murmured, not
long before the end, as his thin hand had passed over
her hair.

'It was good enough for you though,' she'd said stubbornly and tearfully.

'That's because I . . . experimented before I chose this. And so should you. Then, if you find you still want it, come back.'

'They . . . think I'm a freak down there, though.'

'No. Not the real people. They won't. Go and see Alex Cameron. He'll help you with a job, other things too. He's a real person and besides, he owes me a favour . . .'

Well I did that, Hannah thought, still studying her hands. I knocked back all those kind, kind offers to take me in and I came down here fully intending to ask this man to help me find a job but instead of finding a . . . father-like figure, like the Reverend Clayton, I found something else. Something I don't quite understand. Something that makes it impossible to . . . to . . .

She looked up suddenly into those dark, watchful eyes.

'What else did that fancy school teach you?' he asked thoughtfully.

'To type, to—well, a basic secretarial course, to sew and cook, how to walk and dress. How to give a dinner party, the art of conversation . . . all that kind of stuff.'

He grinned and murmured, 'Perhaps more useful than you give it credit for, Hannah, although, not necessarily if you intend to bury yourself beyond the Barcoo tending someone else's infants. Tell me though, did you never think to put some part of this education you acquired so painfully, to better use? Especially the commercial side of it?'

'Yes, I did,' she said and frowned because she had applied for quite a few jobs since she'd been staying with the Claytons. 'Lack of previous experience is the greatest problem. Although how one is supposed to have had it when you're only eighteen and have not long left school is a bit of a mystery to me.'

'Well, a lot of girls leave school when they're fifteen or sixteen, you see. So by the time they're eighteen, they have a head start on someone like you. All the same,' he narrowed his eyes suddenly, 'I'm sure you have talents they don't—if you're anything like your father,' he said slowly.

'What do you mean?'

'Do you know much about horses, Hannah?'

'Well, quite a lot. He ... taught me a lot about them, too. And I love them. Why do you ask?'

Alex Cameron was silent for a time. Then he said wryly, 'I'll never laugh at Providence again. The thing is, Hannah, the reason why you found it so difficult to get through to me, and for that matter, why the office is in such a mess ... you might have noticed?'

'Well ... yes.'

'The reason for it all is that I lost a rather key member of my staff a short time ago. I used to call her my Girl Friday although she was in her fifties. But she used to handle a lot of the stuff Sylvia is now having to wade through, but at home. You see, I have this place at Nerang where the actual sales are conducted.' He went on to explain about his home. 'She also sort of supervised the overall running of the place although she didn't live in ... But you could.'

'I ...' Hannah blinked. 'Do you mean you're offering me—that job?'

'Yes I am. I've had an employment agency looking for someone, so far with no success. I mean I can get typists who don't have the slightest idea what they're typing when it comes to a ... yearling catalogue for example and I can get out-of-work show jumpers who can't type, although they know horses backwards. In you though, I'd have both those skills, plus someone who can help out with the entertaining I do.' He smiled suddenly. 'So you'd be able to put *all* your skills to work.'

'I ... I mean, I'm amazed,' Hannah said faintly, when she finally found her voice.

He regarded her quizzically. 'Are you? Thinking back, Hannah, I can't help recalling what you said to me in the lift.'

'W-what?' Hannah asked nervously.

He stretched out his long legs and his eyes glinted wickedly for a moment, before he said gravely, 'You said something about ... that you were trying to see someone—who we've now established was me—not *exactly* on a business matter. Does that mean it was and it wasn't or—half and half?' he queried.

Hannah bit her lip. 'Well,' she said, then stopped.

'You mentioned something else,' he murmured. 'About wearing your best dress to impress—me, I take it?' His eyes suddenly quizzed hers acutely. 'Did you also want to ask me to help you get a job, Hannah, but because of what happened yesterday, you changed your mind?'

'Oh,' Hannah said at last, and controlled an urge to bite her nails—a habit she thought she'd cured herself of, 'yes. But I didn't expect *you* to give me a job.'

'Why not? Seeing as there's one available. I can assure you, Hannah, what happened in the lift was not the way I go about business. Nor was it the way I would dream of treating a daughter of William Hawthorn's. Only I didn't know. As a matter of fact,' he said, with a sudden gleam of laughter in his eye, 'I don't generally go about doing that kind of thing at all. It must be something to do with getting *stuck* in lifts— perhaps it produces strange impulses in people!'

Hannah thought of her own frantic reaction and had to laugh a little then. 'Yes,' she said ruefully. Then she looked at him very seriously. 'If you're sure you're not just being ... well, charitable?' she said tremulously.

'Ask Sylvia!' he replied with a grin. 'Actually, if you'd like to spend a few days in the office with her first, while you think it over before you move out, it'll give you a fair idea of how we do things ...'

CHAPTER TWO

'WELL,' Hannah said, later that same day to the Reverend and Mrs Clayton, 'he lives at Nerang and he has this big complex there—a sales ring for his thoroughbred auctions, stabling for horses that pass through the sales and his own training track and training establishment too. From what I can gather it's like a small community actually. He has his own house and there are cottages on the property for his trainer and other staff . . .'

'Of course!' Mrs Clayton said. She turned to her husband. 'You know it, dear. I must say it's all very impressive and it's right out in the country. I mean it's in a lovely bush setting although,' she pondered, 'at most it would be only half an hour's drive from here. Go on, Hannah.'

'Well, he had someone out there who used to deal with the paper work involving the horses that passed through and . . . used to co-ordinate the running of the place. Only she had to leave unexpectedly and he wants someone to replace her, someone who knows horses and . . . well, he does a lot of entertaining of southern buyers and racing people and it would be part of the job to help organise that. I could live there, although the last person didn't, but she lives at Nerang.'

There was a small silence. Then Ted Clayton said, 'Is he married?'

'I didn't ask,' Hannah replied. 'Probably not or he'd have mentioned it. I'd have my own cottage next door

28

to his trainer who *is*, and has five children. Mr
Cameron says he has a housekeeper for his own house.
What do you think?' she asked breathlessly.

The Reverend Clayton studied her expectant face
and mused inwardly and quite unexpectedly that he
was very glad he didn't have an eighteen year old
daughter himself—particularly one as fresh and
innocent looking as Hannah. Then he thought with a
certain wryness, that if Alex Cameron had been
married, he probably would have given his unqualified
approval yet it often meant little or nothing these days.
So what am I trying to say to myself? he wondered. I
don't know a great deal about the man but I do know a
fair bit about the kind of society he moves in. Wealthy,
sophisticated ... He came out of his reverie with a
start to see Hannah looking at him and he got the
impression she was reading his mind fairly accurately.

Which was confirmed when she said a little
hesitantly, 'My father counted him as a great friend. I
don't think you need to ... to worry about him ...'
She stopped uncertainly.

'Do you want to take this job, Hannah?' he asked
quietly.

'I think so,' Hannah said. 'I'd like to prove I could
handle it. Actually, it would be like a dream come
true,' she added candidly.

'If I said that it's a very different world to the one
you're used to, would you think I was an old stick in
the mud?'

'No,' Hannah said consideringly. 'I'd think you're
probably quite right. And very kind and very sweet
to—to worry about me. I also think I have to take the
plunge sometime, though.' She looked at him very
directly.

'Then you have my blessing on one proviso, my dear.

That you look upon Mrs Clayton and myself as family and treat us as such.'

Several minutes later when Hannah had left, brushing away some happy tears, Mrs Clayton looked at her husband and detected an expression in his eye that she knew well. She said, 'You'll go and see him, I suppose. She might not like that . . .'

'There's no reason she should know.'

'Do you think it's wise to interfere, though, Ted? I think she's struggling desperately to be . . . grown up and independent.'

'I'm not going to interfere, my dear,' her husband said. 'I shall simply pay a call on him to introduce myself and to let him know that Hannah is not quite alone in the world. There can be no harm in that. He might have been a great friend of her father's but he's still a man.'

Mrs Clayton sighed. 'I still can't believe how very lovely Hannah has grown up to be, you know. The thing is, I don't think she realises it, or the kind of *impact* it can have, rather.'

'All the same, there's a good side to that,' the Reverend Clayton said musingly. 'She's not a silly young thing with only that on her mind exactly, is she?'

'Oh no,' Mrs Clayton agreed. 'Far from it. But something I've observed in my quite long life now, is the fact that the kind of—I suppose you could call it innocence—Hannah possesses, is a very potent form of attraction in itself. I won't say any more otherwise you'll be rushing out to buy a shotgun. We shall just have to trust in the Lord.'

'That's my line,' Ted Clayton said with a grin and pinched her cheek affectionately.

*   *   *

Two months later, Hannah woke up one morning to the startling realisation that she'd grown into her new life so thoroughly, it was hard to imagine any other.

She lay quite still in bed and listened to the birdsong and thought of the early sunlight filtering through the gum leaves to catch the dew on the tall grass of the bushland surrounding the property. She thought too of the cool and mysterious green of the hills beyond, that rose up to places with fascinating names like Binna Burra and the Lamington Plateau and Mount Lindsay and Mount Warning.

Then the thud of hoofbeats claimed her attention and she knew she was late for the track work session that took place at the Cameron establishment six days a week without fail. For once, though, she decided to take the time to lie in bed and just think; of so many things, like the smooth turf of the track with its white wooden railing, the sweep of the driveway beyond that led from the big double gates with its border of brilliant flower beds, the stately main house and the huge old peppercorn tree around which the other three cottages were situated.

If one saw the place from the air, she thought, you'd get a dazzling impression of green and white. All the buildings were painted white and there was a lot of money spent on paint. Then there was the green of the track and the sweep of the lawns around the sales ring and the dozen or so neatly fenced paddocks. There was no doubt it was a magnificent property.

It was more too, she mused. It was a community of its own—or rather, like one big family, and if she'd been a successful 'Girl Friday' she'd also become a lot more. She'd been absorbed into the family, an intriguing and diverse family at that!

She thought with affection of her immediate

neighbours, Mick and Marge Riley. Mick was Alex's stable foreman and trainer and in Alex's absence the ultimate authority on any horse that passed through the property. He was a quiet man who was also the ultimate authority in the cheerful bedlam that reigned in his home which included five children, ranging from sixteen to six, and his madcap wife, Marge, who, he often said, was as much of a handful as any of his kids.

Beyond the Riley establishment lived Tom and Jean Watson with two children and the young jockey who was apprenticed to Mick, Billy Johnson. Tom Watson was a farrier by trade, also a horse dentist and handyman—a lean stringy man by contrast to his wife Jean, who was a large, formidable woman and possibly the only person on earth young Billy Johnson was a little in awe of.

The final member of the permanent staff was a Mrs Hunter, the lady who ran the main house and had her quarters in it and in consequence was occasionally moved to feel she was a cut above the others, but, as Marge Riley had predicted to Hannah, once you got to know Mrs Hunter, she did soften.

Hannah sat up and stretched and thought about her employer and her job. She had her own office in the main house next door to Alex's study and so far she thought she'd pleased him with her work, which mainly consisted of co-ordinating the smooth running of every aspect of the property. Not quite as simple as it looks, she mused.

For one thing she had a projected budget to stick to and all the book work associated with it—all the feed bills to pay from the horses to grocery bills for humans. She had to liaise with Mrs Hunter over the matter of entertaining, to familiarise herself with the horses going through the various sales so she could

show them to prospective buyers knowledgeably when
Mick and Tom were otherwise engaged ... In fact
there's enough work to keep me occupied from dawn
to dusk and then some, she thought contentedly.

Another thing she often did, although she was too
late for it this morning, was, because of her light
weight, to ride trackwork for Mick.

As for Alex Cameron, she'd inevitably got to know
him a lot better and in the process discovered some
things about him that were not immediately apparent
on the surface. One of them being that he could
change his personality to suit varying situations, or so
it seemed. Put him in among a crowd of racing people
and he fitted so well you'd imagine he never thought
of anything else. Put him with up-country people with
their broad hats and slow drawls and you'd imagine
he'd never left the Barcoo.

Yet in his own study, on those warm scented
evenings when Hannah first came to work for him, he
was something else again. He read a lot, the kind of
books her father had loved to read and he listened to
music on his hi-fi. Hannah had spent a couple of
evenings with him, reminiscing about the west, as she
knew it so well too. He showed her his fine collection
of Australian paintings as well as the objects he'd
brought home from his apparently frequent trips
overseas, like a gold Russian ikon and a beautifully
engraved brass bowl from India—all of which made
Hannah green with envy.

There was another side to him that she perceived
only gradually. He quite often spent a night away from
home with no explanation and it wasn't until she saw
him one day in Surfer's, quite by accident—it was her
day off—with a beautiful blonde woman who was
looking up at him in a particular way, that things fell

into place—including Mrs Hunter's peculiar expressions of disapproval that always followed these nights away from home. Looks that Alex Cameron either ignored or received with cool amusement.

She must be his mistress, Hannah thought, the blonde woman, and she couldn't help feeling a tinge of envy. Not that she herself had any desire to be anyone's mistress, but she'd been so very elegant and confident looking, the blonde woman.

But the final side to Alex Cameron's personality was the one that Hannah had come into conflict with a couple of times . . .

'As only any right-minded person would,' she mused aloud to herself that morning. The first of those 'run-ins' with her employer came back to her in the form of a vivid mental picture. It started over a stray dog . . .

'Hannah! If you're responsible for the presence of this mongrel will you kindly get rid of him *forthwith*, as your father would have said.'

Hannah looked down at the unprepossessing, shivering little dog in her arms. It had just been rescued with the aid of almost the entire staff, from one of the Alsatian guard dogs which patrolled the stables.

She raised her head and said clearly, 'My father would have said nothing of the kind. The dog is lost. He has no home . . .'

'Then ring up the R.S.P.C.A. and find him a home. He can't stay here,' Alex Cameron said, with cold finality.

'Why not? I'd look after him. I rather like him.'

Alex compressed his lips and turned to Mick Riley. 'Mick, is it not a fact that this same dog ran on to the track this morning and nearly brought down Tiara Tahiti?'

'Sure did,' Billy Johnson remarked, with a reminiscent look on his rather wizened little face. 'Don't know how I kept her on her feet,' he added immodestly. Whatever he lacked in inches and otherwise, Billy had a large and not altogether misplaced confidence in his riding abilities.

'I was talking to Mick,' Alex said coolly.

Mick Riley chewed his lip. 'Well, yes he did,' he said, and wondered what his wife Marge would say to him. Because she'd made no secret that she was exceedingly taken up with Hannah Hawthorn and had even collaborated in the matter of smuggling the stray dog Hannah had found, on to the premises.

'Mick,' Hannah appealed directly, 'we could train this dog, couldn't we?'

Mick pulled a face. 'I doubt it, Hannah. I reckon it's always going to be a pure nuisance to us. It just don't understand horses. You know how you see some dogs that don't have any traffic sense? They get out in the middle of the road, although they must be able to hear you coming, then they look surprised when you run 'em down. This dog'll be the same I reckon.'

'No,' Hannah said stubbornly, and stroked the small trembling body gently.

'Mick's right, Hannah,' Alex said brusquely. 'You'd only be condemning it, and yourself, to a life of misery. Don't you see that?' he added impatiently.

'It's so . . . forlorn, though. It trusts me, I know it does.'

'But not enough to obey you, obviously.'

Hannah raised her eyes and they were stormy. 'How could you be so cruel? The R.S.P.C.A. will only put it down.'

Alex looked at the dog and the fact that he thought it quite likely showed plainly in his eyes and caused

Hannah to say with intense feeling, 'If you make me do this I shall never speak to you again! I . . .'

'Hannah!' Alex Cameron's voice cracked like a whip. Then he turned his head to his wildly interested, assembled staff and said silkily, 'I don't know why you lot are hanging around. We're behind schedule as it is.'

They all melted away immediately, leaving Hannah to her fate and he studied her for a long moment, his eyes hard and cold. Then something in his face changed and he said quietly, 'The dog has to go, Hannah. But I'll ring them personally and ask them to find a home for it. Give it to me.'

'Do you mean that?' she asked with sudden tears in her eyes. 'You're not just saying it, do you promise?'

Alex raised his eyes heavenwards briefly, but he said, 'You have my word.'

Hannah looked down at the dog and then handed it to him. He accepted the small weight from her, and watched her as she hurried away . . .

But the next incident had been infinitely more embarrassing for Hannah, not only because it put her in a ridiculous position, but earned her a thorough scolding as well and, as she sat up in bed, she wondered if she would ever forget the indignity of having to ring her employer from that place of all places . . .

'Hannah!' Alex's voice had come down the line. 'Where the devil are you? I've been trying to get hold of you for hours. I've got a mob of buyers arriving from Hong Kong this afternoon . . . are you back home now?'

'No, Alex. I'm—actually I'm at the Southport Police Station.'

'What the hell are you doing there? Whatever it is, leave it and get home. Mrs Hunter isn't there either.'

'I know. But that's the problem, Alex, I can't get home,' she said in a small voice.

There was a sudden, pregnant silence. Then her employer said, 'All right, hit me with it.'

Hannah flinched. 'It was like this. I was driving into Nerang this morning when I saw this man abusing his horse. I think the horse might have thrown him, but all the same he was poking it in the eye with his whip and hitting it over the head!'

'So you stopped and tried to reason with the man?' Alex Cameron's tones were cool and resigned.

'Yes,' she said meekly, and added honestly, 'only that seemed to make him even more furious. By the way, there was a police car approaching at the time, although I didn't see it then . . .' She broke off and bit her lip.

'Go on.'

Hannah looked at the receiver, then put it reluctantly back to her mouth. 'Well, the man turned on me then and, although he swears now he wouldn't have done it, I thought he was going to hit me with the whip. By the way, the police car had stopped then, although . . .'

'You didn't notice that either,' he supplied. 'Go on . . .'

'S-so, I ducked and the man fell over and stunned himself and the horse pulled free and bolted into the road.'

'I see!' her employer said. 'And how many people were killed?' he enquired conversationally. 'Or was it just the horse?'

'No one was killed!' she said indignantly. 'No one was hurt even and the horse is fine—as fine as it will ever be with an owner like that, at least!'

'So what's the problem then, Hannah?'

Hannah sighed. 'There was another car coming along when the horse bolted, and it swerved to miss the horse and ... ran into the back of the police car ...'

There was a curious silence until Alex Cameron said, 'All right. What have they charged you with?'

Hannah's eyes flashed suddenly and she cast a furious look at the stoical sergeant who stood beside her. 'They can't find anything to charge me with ... with which to charge me,' she said crossly. 'And they won't even charge *him* with cruelty to animals. All they'll say is next time I should mind my own business. But you see we all ended up here at the police station—they made me come with them in the police car ...'

'So it still goes?'

'Yes! But ... it does have a big dent in the back. Well I don't have a cent on me and everyone at home seems to be out so I ... well I thought I'd ring you at the office. I was only going up to collect the mail, you see. I'm really sorry to inconvenience you like this ...'

'So you should be,' he retorted, but with something like smothered laughter in his voice. 'As soon as we get home you're going to have to work like hell because my Hong Kong buyers are staying the night. There are three of them ...'

Hannah suppressed a groan.

Despite that laughter she'd thought she'd detected in his voice, Alex had delivered a rather scathing lecture on the way home, on the impropriety of interfering with other peoples' affairs—to which she'd listened meekly and kept her thoughts on the subject to herself. But perhaps he'd guessed them anyway because he'd said by way of a final shot, 'I'm beginning to feel some sympathy for that school you attended. Also, I'm beginning to understand why it was felt necessary to send you there . . .'

One of the nice things about him, though, she reflected, coming out of her reverie, is that he doesn't bear grudges. Although he does treat me like a child of ten sometimes. But my big opportunity to prove myself is coming up with this dispersal sale, the biggest so far I've handled . . .

Her ponderings at this stage were interrupted by a knock on the door and then the sound of impatient footsteps through her small sitting room and into the bedroom.

'Hannah! Aren't you up yet! You lazy old thing.'

Hannah looked ruefully at the bright, young face and tumbled curls of Sally Riley who was just sixteen and could look amazingly schoolgirlish in her school uniform as she was now, and surprisingly grown up when she was experimenting with her mother's make-up. 'I know, I am lazy this morning,' she agreed with a grin. 'I don't know why. You're up very bright and early, though.'

Sally pulled a face. 'Dad,' she said expressively. 'Last night he told Mum the place was like a brothel and had to be cleaned up. Then she asked him how he knew what a brothel looked like anyway and they had a ding-dong fight!' Sally grinned. 'Anyway this morning they still weren't talking, but he pulled us all out of bed at the crack of dawn to help her which *she* says is worse than having to do it herself. Actually I don't know why they bother. Give it two days and it'll be back as untidy as ever again . . . What I wanted to ask you, though, is that it's Friday and Mum said we could have a barbecue down by the creek tonight, all of us, will you come?' she finished, breathlessly.

'I . . .'

'Oh, don't say you've got something on up at the house,' Sally wailed. 'I was hoping you'd bring your guitar and mouth-organ. Mr Watson is bringing his piano-accordion—Hannah, if you can't come I'll just go up and see Alex and . . .'

'You don't have to,' Hannah said. 'I've got tonight off.'

'Oh great,' Sally said exuberantly. 'But that's a thought. I might ask Alex to come. He's super fun . . .'

She broke off and cocked her head at a distant shout. 'That's me. Mum's yelling so I better get back. Will *you* ask him, Hannah? I gotta go . . .' She rolled her eyes expressively. 'See you later, lazy bones, and don't forget to ask him.' She left the house yelling that she was coming in a piercing voice that made Hannah suck her teeth.

The request to invite Alex had come as no surprise to her, for it hadn't taken her long to discover that her boss had a way with children. It had struck a strange warmth into her heart when he'd once complimented her on how she handled them.

He'd said to her one day after she'd been there about a month, 'How's it going, Pied Piper?'

She'd looked around. 'Who me?'

He'd smiled. 'Whenever I see you these days you have a rag-tag trail of children with you. Do you ever feel like the Old Woman who lived in a shoe?'

'Sometimes,' she'd replied with a grin. 'But it gives their mums a break and I like them.'

'I should say it's mutual. You seem to have a rapport with kids, Although I must admit I've heard a strange cacophony of sounds issuing from your place at times . . . as if you and the kids are strangling cats.'

'Oh dear! Is it that bad? The thing is they're all really keen to learn to play my father's guitar and mouth-organ. It could be worse though,' she teased.

'How?'

'It could have been a set of drums . . .'

'God forbid!'

Yes, she thought with a smile, it could be worse.
But if I don't get out of bed and do something . . .

She glanced at her watch and was galvanised into
action.

'So you reckon you've got everything in hand,
Hannah?'

Alex Cameron swung round in his big chair so that
he could see out of his tall study windows which
afforded a wide view of his property.

Hannah sat on the other side of the desk and paged
through her notebook. They were discussing the
dispersal sale of a famous stud, which was to be
conducted on the following Tuesday. All the horses
had arrived and on Sunday and Monday the Cameron
establishment was to be thrown open to the public and
prospective buyers to enable them to view the horses.

'I . . . I think *so*,' Hannah said, making a note. 'I've
organised the refreshments and the marquee for
Tuesday and chivvied up the catering company and
consulted with Mrs Hunter on the private luncheon
you're giving and so on. The toilets are all working
and—oh, by the way, Billy asked me to let you know
there are two changes to the catalogue. One mare
slipped her foal last night and another that was
supposed to be in foal, apparently isn't. I've typed up
the amendments.'

He turned back from the window and smiled at her.
'Very efficient, Miss Hawthorn,' he commented.

'Thank you,' Hannah said, 'but I guess the proof
will be in the pudding. I mean, if you can still say that
afterwards, that will be the true test.'

He laughed. 'I guess you're right . . .' He cast her a suddenly speculative look. 'Been having any more trouble with a . . . certain admirer, shall we say?'

Hannah looked away and felt a slow colour burn in her cheeks because, for reasons beyond her comprehension, Billy Johnson had developed a crush on her, despite the fact that he was nearly twelve months younger and a good three inches shorter than she was. Nothing she said or did made the slightest difference. He was always pestering her to go to the drive-in with him, bringing her floral tributes, which he culled from the flowerbeds that bordered the driveway, whistling at her as she walked past—and once, had even provoked her into slapping his face.

All of which annoyed her immensely. She'd never before had any trouble keeping young men at bay, and having to resort to face slapping wasn't quite in keeping with the sophisticated image she was trying to project.

Perhaps the most annoying thing of all, though, had been the fact that Alex Cameron had been an unseen witness when she'd slapped Billy's face and he'd only revealed himself after Billy had stalked off, and then laughed with considerable enjoyment until she'd retreated too, in high dudgeon.

'No,' she said shortly. 'Besides, don't you know it's bad manners to eavesdrop on people?'

'Do you class that as eavesdropping?' he asked with a glint in his eye. 'I would have thought the opposite. I doubt if you could have chosen a more public spot and anyone who happened to be within earshot would have had to be deaf to have missed it.'

Hannah set her jaw and stared back at him resolutely because sometimes there was something infinitely infuriating about Alex Cameron—part of which, she realised angrily, was his sheer, undeniably attractive maleness. He might be old enough to be her father and have a sprinkling of grey in his dark hair and those deceptively sleepy eyes, but there was also something about the way his tall strong body moved that made her catch her breath sometimes. And occasionally, just the sight of his lean, brown hands lying on the desk had the same effect on her. While she'd accepted the fact that this was probably only what a lot of females of the species might suffer when confronted with her worldly, wealthy employer and hadn't allowed herself to dwell on it particularly, it suddenly irked her strangely, for that very reason, to think of him being amused in a highly adult way at what she was going through with Billy.

While all this shot through her mind, he took advantage of the pause to say, 'Don't you think you're being a little hard on him?'

Hannah opened her mouth in surprise—something he took further advantage of to add wryly, 'I'm told it can make life hell—falling in love. Without getting your face slapped into the bargain.' His eyes danced wickedly.

Hannah shut her mouth with a click then took a deep breath and said sweetly, 'If you're only going on hearsay, I'm surprised you feel able—rather *constrained*, to offer me advice.'

He burst out laughing to say finally and appreciatively, '*Touché*, Hannah. All the same I still can't help feeling a bit sorry for Billy. You'd think for his first taste of the old Adam and Eve business, he'd have found himself someone of his own fighting weight. Some sweet little girl who would have reciprocated his admiration instead of a sharp-tongued, fiery creature like yourself—a prim and proper do-gooder into the bargain, who's also very handy with her fists.'

'*Oh*,' Hannah breathed, so outraged it took a mighty effort to control an impulse to launch herself at him with those same fists.

To make matters worse he simply sat back and observed her inward struggle with a look of detached interest added to his amusement. And by the time Hannah had counted to ten beneath her breath and rather mangled her notebook instead, he said mildly, 'Very wise.'

'What do you mean?' she asked, through gritted teeth.

He raised an eyebrow mockingly. 'That you wouldn't find it nearly so easy to put me in my place as Billy.'

'I . . . all right!' She stood up furiously. 'I must say I'm surprised though, to hear you admit you need putting in your place—almost as surprised, that is, as to hear your sentiments on the subject of Billy. Would you rather I encouraged him and then slapped him? If you'd heard what he said to me . . .'

'I did,' he drawled. 'He complimented you on a certain portion of your anatomy in a rather vulgarly worded, but none-the-less genuine manner.' He grinned suddenly. 'He only spoke the truth. You do have . . . a beautiful figure, Hannah, but before you expire from rage,' he looked at her stunned, scarlet face quizzically, 'I agree with you—it's entirely your own business until you choose to make it otherwise. I'm just surprised, in view of your extreme sympathy for stray dogs and abused horses, that you couldn't have gone about it a bit differently. In case you don't realise it, when you're a boy and seventeen and only five foot two, you're horribly vulnerable. Although Billy would die rather than let anyone know it.'

Hannah had been in the act of walking out, but she

turned at his words and her eyes sought his, and she
was shocked to see that for once, he was quite serious.

She sat down again rather abruptly. 'I didn't think
of it that way,' she said very slowly. 'You don't think
he's feeling this . . . seriously, though, do you?'

Alex Cameron studied her thoughtfully. 'I don't
suppose it will be a life long passion with him,
although your first love can be . . . sort of special. And
you have to give him credit for perseverance in face of
enormous odds.'

'Thank you,' Hannah said ironically. Then she
looked at him helplessly. 'What *do* I do? I . . . I mean
it's never really happened to me before.'

'Never?' he queried with a probing look.

'Well, no. You see, all the boys I ever knew, *knew*
who I was, the minister's daughter, and so when they
saw I wasn't interested, they . . . *didn't* persevere.
Besides, until not so very long ago, no one in their
right minds would have looked at me twice.'

Alex lifted his eyebrows in a momentary expression
of disbelief.

'It's true,' Hannah confided. 'I had braces on my
teeth that I often thought looked as if they could have
guarded Fort Knox, and I seemed to be all hands and
feet then—you know, clumsy and uncoordinated, and
I was always speaking my mind, as well as knocking
things over and tripping around the place and . . .' She
stopped and coloured faintly.

'Go on.'

'I was thin,' she said wryly. 'When I was fifteen
every other girl I knew was . . . looked like a girl, while
I was still like a piece of four by two. Like a plank, in
other words,' she added for his edification.

'I've seen a few pieces of four by two in my time,'
he murmured, and his lips twitched in that disconcert-

ing manner she'd observed before. He said, 'What do you think wrought the difference?'

'I've wondered about that,' she replied candidly. 'There's nothing I can put my finger on though, so I suppose I was just a late developer—like the ugly duckling. But to get back to Billy,' she said seriously. 'Now I stop to think about it, I guess I could have been more tactful. Only . . . but you're right,' she added with sudden determination. 'I . . .'

'What were you going to say?' he interrupted her curiously. 'Only . . .?'

She shrugged. 'I only wondered if there *was* a way to be more tactful about these things without . . . without . . .'

'Being misunderstood?' he offered, his eyes glinting suddenly.

'Well, yes,' she said. 'What do you think?'

He lay back in his chair and for just a moment Hannah got the oddest feeling he was looking right through her and not seeing her at all, but something curiously satirical. Then those dark eyes were amused again and his fingers released the pen he'd been holding so that it clattered to the desk and he said pensively, 'I'm sure if I was your father, I'd advise you to be very wary of being—misunderstood, in that line, because it's an area where a girl can run into all sorts of problems. So, speaking for your father, I'd say you're on the right track. It's only that Billy doesn't seem to me to be enough of a real threat for you to be so dedicated about it. In fact, when he's not trying to . . . chat you up, when you're riding together for example, you get on quite well, don't you? I mean he does have a sense of humour, doesn't he?'

'Yes . . . So you think I should have him for a friend?' she asked doubtfully.

'Why not? You can handle him.' He swung his chair round to look out of the window for about a minute, and then he turned back to her and there was something strangely sober in his eyes as he said, 'But there'll be others, Hannah. And they'll be men, not boys. I've seen a few of them eyeing you already.'

She blinked.

He smiled crookedly. 'Save your energy for fighting them off, Hannah. Eighteen is awfully young to get— entangled with anyone, but not too young to come ... under siege. Especially in the kind of world you're moving in now and with the kind of very experienced men you're meeting. Besides,' he sat up and looked at her humorously, 'I'd hate to lose my secretary now I've broken her in.'

Hannah digested this in silence and with a look of discomfort. Then she said after a while, 'About Billy. I really feel bad now. Maybe if I adopted a sisterly approach ... maybe he'd like to learn to play the guitar!' she added brightening somewhat. 'And talking of guitars, you're invited to a barbecue tonight.' She explained and added ruefully, 'I gather Mick is playing the heavy-handed father at the moment too, so it should come as some light relief for the kids. Will you come?'

'Too?' he queried, ignoring her question. 'Is that what you think I'm doing, playing the heavy-handed father?'

Hannah frowned and went a little pink. 'I didn't mean it to sound like that. I ... appreciate your advice and concern, really I do! But I don't think there's much danger of me falling by the wayside because I'm enjoying life so much just as it is. I feel as if I'm achieving something, earning my own living and so on—well, thanks to you really, but all the same ...

You *were* right about one thing though, it's all very well to worry about stray dogs and the like, but a great mistake not to extend it to people. I shan't fall into that trap again.' She stopped and looked at him with a sudden glint of mischief in her eye. 'Would you like to have a small wager with me?'

He looked at her warily. 'What did you have in mind?'

'That Billy Johnson will get over me completely in the near future, but in a nice way on my part. You see, it's like a challenge now and I can never resist a challenge.' She stood up and grinned at him. 'You haven't told me whether you're coming tonight or not?'

His lips twitched as he looked up at her and he ignored her question momentarily again as he said, 'You're a very sweet chip off the old block, Hannah. Yes I will come tonight, but I might bring someone with me. I don't suppose that will cause any problems?'

'I shouldn't think so,' Hannah said lightly. 'If there's nothing more to do here, I might go and have my lunch.'

She left him staring at the door as it closed behind her and didn't see the rather wry grimace that crossed his face.

CHAPTER THREE

'I WONDER who he's bringing?' Marge Riley said thoughtfully.

She'd abandoned her flurry of spring-cleaning at Hannah's invitation and assurance that her Lord and Master had gone into Southport and would not be back for a few hours, and she was sharing Hannah's lunch with her.

'Who?' Hannah asked as she poured the tea. 'Mick's not bringing anyone, I told you, he's gone into . . .'

'Not Mick,' Marge interrupted crossly. 'Do me a favour and don't mention his name for a while, because I'm not speaking to him just yet. Anyone would think,' she said darkly, 'it was entirely my fault that we have five children and from the way he carries on, anyone would think he was the only tidy person in the world! No, I meant Alex. I wonder who he's bringing to the barbecue?'

'He didn't say,' Hannah replied and eyed her harassed next door neighbour with affection. '*I* think you're marvellous, by the way. I think you cope wonderfully and I'm sure Mick does too, underneath.'

Marge started to say something cutting, but changed her mind suddenly and giggled. 'You know what made it all worse? This morning he couldn't find a brush or a comb. Not *one*, although there must be dozens in the house. And he really looked funny with his hair sticking up all over the place and . . . I laughed, which really sent him ranting and raving! But to get back to Alex. I think there's a new lady in his life. Mick reckons she was with him and Matt Bartholomew at the races, a few weeks back.' Marge allowed an expression of distaste to creep into the way she said the name of Matt Bartholomew.

'Matt . . . is he that tall man with the red hair who's out here quite often?' Hannah asked. 'Lately, anyway?'

'That's him,' Marge said with a suddenly significant look that Hannah missed. 'A right bastard with women he's supposed to be, too.'

'Why does he come out here so often?'

'He owns a half share in Tiara Tahiti for one thing,' Marge answered and seemed about to say something more on the subject of Matt Bartholomew but reverted to the topic of Alex instead and his new girlfriend. 'Trouble is,' she finished finally, 'very few women can resist Alex, you know, but what they don't realise is that he lost his heart once, a long time ago, and he has no intention of doing it again.'

'What do you mean?' Hannah asked curiously.

Marge reached for the teapot. 'It was like this. When he came down from the west, he didn't have much going for him, but a burning ambition to make good. By the time he'd been down here a couple of years he got himself a job as a foreman in a racing stable and, unfortunately, as it turned out, fell in love with one of the owner's daughters. She fell for him too, but her mama and papa—you can't really blame them I suppose—had other ideas. They had Alex sacked and took her off to Europe for twelve months and when they got back, married her off to some nob who'd inherited a grazing empire and been to all the right schools. Well, Alex took it really hard, but it did have a good side to it, I guess. It made him more than ever determined to make good. Which he did.' Marge waved a hand expressively. 'Ever since, though, he's never let himself get trapped into falling in love, although there've been plenty of women in his life.'

'Because he still loves her, do you think?' Hannah asked.

'I reckon so,' Marge commented and munched her sandwich thoughtfully. 'Of course, fifteen years is a long time to carry a torch for anyone, but when you see how good he is with kids and so on, it makes you wonder. Mick reckons that's the only time he's seen Alex get blind drunk, the day he read in the paper that Alison Fairleigh had married someone else.'

Hannah sat quiet, thinking of this new and unexpected side to her boss. She couldn't help shivering slightly as she recalled his words of only that morning ... sometimes your first love can be very special. So he did know what he was talking about, she thought. She said slowly, 'You might be right. Have you known him all that time?'

'Since I married Mick. Mick's known him longer. They more or less grew up together, out west. He was as wild as a kid could be, according to Mick. Funny, isn't it? You wouldn't believe it now, would you? Except, just sometimes, when he gets mad you get the feeling—it's hard to explain, but you get the feeling Alex is capable of doing anything. Not that he ever does, but all the same it's as if there's a little part of him that no one has managed to tame.'

'How old is Alex?' Hannah asked after a time. 'I can't quite make up my mind.'

'Thirty-seven or thereabouts.'

'I thought so,' Hannah said, 'but I wasn't sure.'

Marge looked up.

'Well,' Hannah said ruefully, 'he did once tell me he was old enough to be my father.' She described the incident in the lift to Marge.

'You poor thing!' Marge said when she'd stopped laughing heartily. 'That's nearly as bad as the horse and the police car—sorry, I shouldn't have reminded you of that!' she added, still chuckling, but couldn't resist the rider, 'What you need is a keeper, Hannah!'

'Thanks!' Hannah smiled wryly.

'And technically, he was right,' Marge went on. 'He is old enough to be your father.'

'He certainly acts like my father and my keeper sometimes,' Hannah conceded. 'Between him and the Reverend Clayton—well, they make a good pair.'

'Ah, well,' Marge said philosophically, 'that's all to the good if you ask me. When I see the way . . .' She stopped abruptly.

'What?'

'Nothing,' Marge said slowly then changed her mind. 'Hannah, you want to watch out, pet. Don't think I'm being an old fuddy-duddy when I say this, but you are only eighteen and I don't think you realise how . . . Put it this way, you might not even have known who he was, but I saw Matt Bartholomew watching you the other day when he thought no one was looking and . . .' She hesitated.

'And what?' Hannah asked.

Marge chewed her lip. 'Take it from me,' she said finally, 'he had an . . . unmistakable look in his eye. He's bad news, Hannah.'

Hannah looked astonished. 'I think you're all imagining things,' she said at last. 'Really, you don't need to worry. I've got no intention of getting mixed up with anything like that, and anyway,' she gestured helplessly, 'well, I don't even think about it. Do you know what I mean?'

Marge cocked her head to one side and said consideringly, 'Yes. That's part of the problem,' she added, unconsciously echoing Mrs Clayton's sentiments on the subject. 'You see, men get a great kick out of thinking they're going to be the one to initiate you to all the sweet mysteries of love—for want of a better word,' she said, a trifle cynically. 'It's like a goad to them or a challenge.'

Hannah opened her mouth, but closed it almost immediately as two thoughts slid across her mind. Her own words uttered earlier on the subject of challenges, and the fact that she hadn't been quite honest with Marge or herself. Because she did sometimes think about it. This nebulous subject that seemed to be cropping up in her life too frequently these days, and so unsought. Only never in relation to any of the men—or boys—who were eyeing her allegedly and in reality, but, as she'd realised earlier, just sometimes with Alex Cameron . . .

Which is odd really, she thought, because even if I occasionally wonder about him not in a . . . fatherly context, he obviously looks upon me as a daughter by proxy and sometimes a tiresome one at that . . .

A look of confusion crossed Hannah's face suddenly, that made Marge Riley feel amazingly maternal. Then she saw Hannah's chin come up and a stubborn light enter her eyes and heard her say, 'I can look after myself, Marge. I've had years of training one way and another—after all, I couldn't have a better moral background, could I? So I don't see why you're all so worried that I'm liable to keel over for the first man I come across.'

Marge shrugged. 'Morals are nothing tangible, love, when someone who knows what he's doing sets out to seduce you. Not that I imagine for one moment that you're liable to keel over for the first man you come across, but,' she sighed suddenly, 'just be careful. I know . . .'

Hannah jumped up. 'I'm tired of this,' she said exasperatedly. 'That's two lectures I've had in the space of a couple of hours. Let's forget it now, shall we?' she pleaded. 'Let's talk about the barbecue . . .'

Marge complied with a grin, although she couldn't help wondering if she'd said too much or not enough.

'That's it!' Hannah protested laughingly. 'I'm totally puffed.'

She looked around in the warm glow of the bonfire, that painted the trunks of two old ghost gums gold and cast a flickering net of the same colour over the creek as it flowed swiftly and silently into the darkness. All about her, flushed laughing faces set up a clamour for more music and Master Richard Watson, who was the youngest child on the property—a five-year-old with a face like an angel and a talent for mischief Hannah had rarely seen equalled—slid into her lap and begged her not to stop playing.

The barbecue had been an unqualified success with every one throwing off their tensions to join in the fun. Tom Watson had constructed an iron grid over a hollow in the ground and upon it, chops and steaks and sausages had sizzled aromatically, to be consumed later with fresh salads and potatoes in their jackets, followed by fruit salad and ice-cream. The children had run races until darkness had fallen and then tried to frighten the lives out of themselves by telling ghost stories. The high point of the evening, however, had come when Hannah had been persuaded to make music alternately on the guitar and mouth-organ, together with Tom on his accordion. Everyone from the oldest to the youngest had danced energetically and some, surprisingly, with more skill than others. Jean Watson had been one of these, amazingly light on her feet for a woman of her bulk, and she'd treated them to a solo horn-pipe which had so inspired Billy Johnson, he'd jumped up and persuaded her to dance a hora with him, for which effort they received great applause, especially when Jean had effortlessly lifted him off his feet and twirled him round and round.

Another of the more skilful dancers had been Alex who'd come on his own after all, and Hannah had watched appreciatively as he'd taught Sally some intricate steps. Then her strumming fingers had faltered for just an instant as she'd seen the laughing, admiring way Sally had looked up at him. And she'd thought—Oops! There goes another heart . . . but she'd shaken herself immediately and wondered what she'd meant by another . . .

All the same, when Mick said that this was all very well, but shouldn't Hannah get a chance to dance too? she'd said laughingly that she was having just as much fun watching them. She'd stuck to that too, despite, or perhaps because of, Billy's look of disappointment, and the fact that she was curiously unwilling to dance with Alex . . .

'Come on, Hannah,' Richard said entreatingly, and touched her face.

'Oh—all right,' she answered and kissed his almost white-blond head. 'Because you've been such a good boy tonight . . .'

'Hear, hear!' his maternal parent remarked feelingly, for none of the awe she was able to inspire in others appeared to be felt by her youngest offspring.

Hannah grinned across at Jean Watson and went on, 'Because you've been such a good boy, I'll play your favourite.'

A collective groan went up. 'You've played *Waltzing Matilda* six times, Hannah!' Billy said.

'Well, let's do it differently,' Hannah said. 'Let's act out the words. We need troopers and a jolly jumbuck . . .'

Richard leapt up, fired with enthusiasm. 'I'm the jolly jumbuck! I'm . . .'

His enthusiasm seemed contagious, so much so that they went through it three times before Hannah and Tom had to stop because they were laughing so much at the antics of the adults, let alone the children.

Alex dropped down beside Hannah finally and said, 'It's all very well for you to laugh, you're not up there making a fool of yourself.'

'I thought you were superb,' she said, wiping her eyes. 'I really thought you were going to jump into the billabong and not be taken alive—said he. The kids loved it.'

He eyed her speculatively. 'I suspect you suggested it for the fun of seeing us all cavorting around like idiots.'

'Not at all!' Hannah denied, but went off into another fit of laughter. 'It just happened that way. Oh dear, now I've got a stitch!'

'Serves you right,' he said cruelly and then threw a casual arm about her and hugged her. 'You've been great tonight . . .'

'Thank you,' she said, 'it's been a great night . . .' Her response, however, was not as casual as he had been because she suddenly found herself feeling shy and breathless in a way that had nothing to do with her laughter at all.

The party began to break up then and, after helping to put an assortment of over excited children to bed and seeing, one by one, the neighbouring lights go off,

Hannah found herself pleasantly weary but not sleepy. She sat on her verandah and watched the stars and the moon and listened to the night sounds and made an astonishing discovery—that she felt curiously lonely, and loath to enter her own empty cottage.

Which is crazy, she told herself. I'm surrounded by people I like, some of whom take so much interest in my welfare as to be a little annoying on occasions.

'But I don't actually belong to anyone and I don't have anyone who belongs to me,' she murmured. 'I mean, I do have relatives in England who sort of disowned my father for choosing to bury himself beyond the black stump, and I suppose I must have some on my mother's side, but no one close, so it's not the same thing. It's just a pity I don't have any brothers or sisters . . .'

'Talking to yourself, Hannah?' a voice said.

She gasped and nearly fainted from fright as a tall figure loomed out of the darkness. 'Who—Alex! What are you doing out there?'

'I decided to check on the horses on the way up.' He leant on the verandah rail and the moonlight picked out the silver in his hair, but cast a shadow on his face. 'I thought you'd be asleep by now.'

'So did I,' she said. 'I . . . I don't know what it is but I just don't feel like going to bed.'

'Then come up and have a night-cap with me. I don't feel like going to bed yet, either.'

'A-all right,' she said after a moment and stood up.

They walked through the citrus grove at the side of the big house and Hannah stopped and sniffed and said, 'Was it your idea to plant orange and lemon trees here?'

He looked across at her. 'Yes. Why?'

'It was a brilliant idea. I often stop and smell the air

here and imagine I'm in some wildly exotic, tropical place like Zanzibar or the Seychelles where you can smell cloves, see flying fish and the sky turn pale green, and taste pomegranates ... Did you perhaps think of that when you planted these trees?'

'Strangely enough, yes.'

'So you've been there?'

'Yes, Hannah.' He reached for her hand. 'Is that one of your ambitions? To go to Africa?'

'Oh yes. Not only Africa, though. I'm constantly lured to Asia too. I'd love to see Mount Everest and the flowers of Nepal and the prayer wheels on the mountain passes, and the burning Deccan Pike. I will too, one day,' she said dreamily, soothed into a mood of romanticism by the moonlight, the perfume on the air and the feel of his hand around hers. Then she laughed and freed her hand. 'I'm getting carried away. I've never told anyone about those dreams. But if you've been there...'

'I've never seen Everest.'

'Oh well, I don't suppose many people do, but it's nice to dream about it.'

They started to walk again and he said presently, 'Is that what you're thinking about when you look through people sometimes and seem to be so unconscious of them?'

'Do I do that? I didn't realise it...'

'Sometimes.'

'It's probably only because I'm concentrating on getting things right,' she said wryly. 'My father used to say to me that I had a one track mind. He used to laugh about it, but I'm sure it can be quite a disability now I come to think of it...'

He looked down at her dark head, with its sleek cap of shining almost blue-black hair, that barely reached his shoulder and grinned to himself. 'Another dragon to slay, Hannah?'

'Yes.' She glanced up at him. 'I'm accumulating quite a list, aren't I? Materialism, treating dogs like people and people like dogs—getting around with a one track mind.' Her face split into a rueful grin. 'Do you ever have these problems?'

'If you mean do I have any besetting sins, yes of course. Some of which may make yours pale by comparison.' His eyes laughed at her. 'For instance, I have a shocking temper, as your father often pointed out to me.'

'Well, he should have known,' Hannah replied, 'because he had a temper himself—at least he claimed he did, but I never really saw it. For that matter, I've seen you angry and cold but never in the grip of a terrible rage. I suppose it's age that does it? Helps you to grow out of these things?'

He laughed with some irony and said wryly, 'Dear Hannah, I sometimes feel like Old Father Time in your company . . .'

She stopped walking and turned to him almost urgently. 'I think that's the biggest problem I have to contend with, you know. I often feel very adult and then someone quite demolishes me so that I feel like a very naïve child. You did it just then. In fact you've done it twice today and Marge had a go at me this morning, too. Am I so . . . so childish?'

The moonlight that had hidden his face from her earlier, showed it to her now in almost stark relief as he stared down at her with his eyes slightly narrowed and his lips faintly twisted. Then he lifted a hand to touch her face, and said with a strange gentleness, 'Yes . . . Not childish but naïve and I think probably, you always will be. Your father was in some ways too, but it can be a very precious commodity when you're also a caring, meticulous, involved person. So you shouldn't worry, Hannah.'

She took a breath and couldn't imagine what compelled her to say then, 'Do you ever feel lonely? Is that . . . childish? That's really why I didn't want to go to bed tonight . . .'

His fingers moved on her face and something in his eyes changed. Then he dropped his hand abruptly and said, 'I know.'

'How did you know?' she asked after a moment, in a slightly husky voice.

'It wasn't hard to work out. Not especially tonight, but when you found it so hard to give up that dog, I realised then what you felt.'

'Oh,' she said in a small voice. 'Only—sometimes it's more than what a pet could . . . could assuage. But actually,' she shrugged and smiled shakily, 'I don't often feel it. I'll survive it. I'm quite tough inside, you know. It must be this moonlight and the scent of the orange trees that's making me maudlin.' Then she yawned surprisingly and grinned. 'There. I think I'll sleep like a log after all!'

He regarded her reflectively then reached out and took her shoulders in his hands.

She looked up at him enquiringly.

'I thought I might be permitted to kiss you good night, in the best, fatherly tradition,' he said gravely. 'You could still come up for a night-cap if you liked but . . .'

She shook her head mutely and it seemed as if they stared into each other's eyes for a small eternity before he gathered her loosely into his arms and bent his head and kissed her lips.

It was barely more than a touching of his lips to

hers, but it seemed to stun Hannah queerly. She found she was afflicted with that same breathlessness as before, but added to it was an astonishing awareness of the lines and curves of her figure and the slightness and softness of it against the hard tautness of his as their bodies rested together briefly and impersonally.

For the first time in her life Hannah felt a sudden comprehension of her femininity; some understanding of what it was to be a woman and that the differences, and the limitations of it which she had often lamented, had a strange power of their own. The power to fill her with a curious headiness and longing that brought its own sense of sadness too, because while she was experiencing a wondrous awakening, she was also, she knew, only a child being kissed good night to him. The bitter and the sweet, she thought dazedly. I never knew . . .

Then he released her and stepped back and she put a hand to her lips in an unconscious gesture of wonder.

Something in his face tightened as he watched and she saw it, and felt all of a sudden supremely uncomfortable and awkward and she snatched her hand away and coloured painfully. Her feet seemed to have lost the power to obey her brain, which was commanding them to run and it wasn't until he said, in a voice that seemed weary and unexpectedly harsh, 'Go to bed, Hannah,' and turned away, that she was released from the spell that seemed to be binding her to the spot, to stumble back to her cottage; to go to bed with her mind blank and numb.

Several days later, however, she was forced to acknowledge that her bright, happy world had become a place of tension and strain. She had tried desperately hard not to dwell on that moonlight kiss, but found it near impossible. Although she strove valiantly to act as if it had never happened, there were times when she couldn't help re-living it in her mind and finding herself trembling and going hot and cold at the thought of anyone, but especially Alex, if he had not already done so, divining the quite undaughterly, not to mention unbusinesslike way she sometimes thought of him now.

If he did though, he gave no sign of it—at least none that Hannah was responsible for. A certain—it was hard to put her finger on it—generally less affable, air about him was the best description she could come up with, and she told herself it was the strain of the major yearling sale that had them all a bit tense and strung-up. Even after the sale had passed, with nothing major going wrong but an obvious down-trend in prices—well I suppose that's worrying for him too, she thought, if it lasts . . .

Another cause for discomfort came from Matt Bartholomew and she found herself wishing heartily that Marge had never said anything about him, because she might then have been able to go about as before, in happy ignorance of his interest which in no way resembled Billy Johnson's cheeky, for-all-to-see method of pursuing her.

Yet it was Billy's own strange behaviour that underlined it, if anything. He began to exhibit an uncharacteristic dislike of the tall, red-headed part-owner of Tiara Tahiti. Uncharacteristic because the filly was the best horse in the racing stable, with apparently unlimited potential and normally under no circumstances would Billy have allowed anything to rock the boat with either of the owners, and thereby jeopardise his chance of sharing a long and illustrious career with the filly.

Hannah, however, could not doubt that he was doing just that—allowing his dislike of Matt Bartholomew to show through, and always contriving to be on the spot whenever Hannah was around. All of which began to take considerable toll of her nerves and she began to understand what Alex had meant when he'd said something about 'coming under siege'.

Yet Matt Bartholomew was never offensive, never *said* anything to make her feel uncomfortable, sometimes made her laugh with his dry wit and it was only the odd, disturbing look in his eyes as they rested on her that made her fluctuate from a state of thinking that Billy was being idiotic and Marge imaginative, to a state of nervous wariness.

Life went on, she discovered, despite these annoyances and frustrations and the times when she was tired and couldn't monitor her thoughts or stop herself from wishing forlornly that she was older and wiser.

Then one day, some weeks later, she found herself looking back on those troubled times and thinking that they'd been a veritable paradise by comparison . . .

It started out like any other day. Clear summer weather, the smell and the sound of horses and the bush, sprinklers netting the green lawns with diamond bright drops of water and a blue, blue sky that made one think of the ocean not so far away.

A small girl had fallen off her bicycle and gashed her knee just as Hannah was driving past on her way home from an early trip into Nerang, to clear the post office box. The child had ripped her school dress and been so considerably shaken up and upset that she couldn't remember her address and didn't even seem to be too sure of her last name. Hannah had put her into the car, a battered little Mini that she usually drove, hidden the bike behind a clump of bushes deciding to do something about it later because there was nowhere to fit it in, and had driven the still sobbing child home with her. There she'd bathed her knee, sewed up her dress, soothed her with a glass of milk and taken her to see the Rileys' aviary which contained a colourful throng of budgerigars, rosellas and canaries. This had so delighted the little girl, she'd quite forgotten her woes and it had taken some time for Hannah to prise her away.

Just how the time had slipped away, only dawned on Hannah when they were back in the car and she switched on the radio and prepared to drive off, but stopped as the implications of a police alert she heard being broadcast, sank in.

She often thought later that it must have been Fate that had seen both Marge and Jean out, and Mick and Tom nowhere to be found and therefore only Alex to turn to . . .

So it happened that she stood in the study of the big house with the bewildered child clutched by the hand and heard Alex say with a kind of infinite weariness as he glanced from her to the little girl, who was crying again, 'What the devil is this? A stray child?'

'Yes . . . *No!* It's like this . . .' She took a breath and explained how she happened to have the child in her company.

'So? What's the problem?' he queried with a hint of impatience. 'You probably should have driven her to school and let them fix her up in case they missed her and got the whole countryside searching for her, but . . .'

'That's just it,' Hannah said jerkily. 'They are. I . . . I heard a police broadcast on the radio. It seems not long after she left home, her mother realised she'd left her lunch behind, so she cadged a lift with their neighbour who was just leaving for work and took the lunch to school. Of course the child hadn't arrived so they went back to look for her and found the bike. Then they called in the police and . . . and now they're broadcasting an alert for fear she's been . . . kidnapped or something horrible and . . . and it's that policeman whose car that got run into the day—*that* day—who is heading the investigation.'

Alex stood up in a swift, lithe movement that reminded Hannah of a tiger about to spring on its prey and she took an involuntary step backwards as he said, 'My God, I don't *believe* you sometimes, Hannah! How long have you had the kid here?'

'I . . . I . . .' she stammered, going paler as she saw the anger in his eyes.

'Never mind,' he said, through his teeth. 'Get in the car. I'll be with you in a minute.' He turned to the phone.

There followed one of the most unforgettable and sickeningly embarrassing episodes of Hannah's life. And it was not much consolation that Alex supported her throughout all her explanations to an irate police sergeant who remembered her only too well, and a distraught mother who swore she'd aged ten years in the space of an hour or so. Not much consolation, because she could still see the barely contained anger in his eyes and somehow it frightened her more than anything else.

When they were back home, after he'd driven them there in a cold silence, she got out of the car and after a moment's hesitation was about to turn away, but he said, 'No you don't. I've got a few things to say to you, Hannah.'

He chose to say them in the privacy of the study and, for the most part, it was a repetition of what he'd said to her once before, only this time it was much stronger, so much so, that she shivered inwardly and it took all her willpower not to burst into tears at his cutting, cruelly harsh words.

Then finally it got too much for her and she tilted her chin, her grey eyes taking on a smouldering look of their own and she said tautly, 'I don't care what you say, that child was too *young* to be riding to school in the first place. She was only a baby and you have no right to swear at me. I . . .'

'It's not *your* business whether she was old enough or not, and why shouldn't I swear at you? You're enough to make a saint swear!' he retorted acidly.

'My father never swore at me.'

'Your father never swore at anyone. It's a pity, however, that he didn't make an exception for you.'

She stared at him and felt her lips tremble. 'W-what did I do that was so very wrong? It was really only an unfortunate coincidence. If the child hadn't left her lunch at home, none of this would have happened. And I still think . . .'

'But the trouble is, you don't, Hannah,' he said savagely. 'That's why nothing is simple when you're involved, because you never stop to think and I'll tell you something else, I'm getting bloody tired of being your guardian angel—you don't need a father! You need a husband who'll keep you too busy in bed and out of it, and who'll give you enough children to satisfy your maternal instincts so you won't have time to vent them on other people's dogs and horses and kids. That's what you need,' he said with his eyes cold and violent.

Her mouth dropped open but he wasn't quite

finished, she found. Because he smiled unpleasantly at her stunned expression and remarked drily, 'Then we all might get some peace around here. Something that is singularly lacking on your account, at present.'

'*Oh!* I . . . well,' she said and dashed at the scalding tears that ran down her cheeks, 'I better do something about that, hadn't I?' With that she turned on her heel, twisting out of the hard hand he put out to stop her, and ran out of the room and out of the house.

I hate you. I *hate* you . . . the words pounded through her brain as she jumped into the Mini car and drove it wildly down the driveway, narrowly missing one of the gateposts. 'How could you say that to me?' she whispered despairingly. 'How could you?'

It was some miles before she stopped to think about where she was going. Then she did a detour which would lead her to the peace and security of the Rectory and the Claytons.

When she arrived, it was only to find no one home, a fact for which she was grateful in an obscure way, as it gave her time to regain some composure and clean up her face. As she sat in the living room waiting for them, knowing they wouldn't mind in the least that she'd used the spare key always left under a pot plant on the verandah, the determination to seek their advice and bare her heart to them grew slowly weaker.

When the Reverend and his wife finally arrived home and delightedly pressed her to have lunch with them and spend the afternoon there, she found it impossible to embark in what now seemed like a tangled tale with not much sense to it.

She did stay, though, and found herself unwittingly soothed by their company. So much so, that by five o'clock, she thought she was restored enough at least, to drive home—although what she was going to do

68 SOME SAY LOVE

when she got there, and how she was going to face Alex again, she had no idea. Nor did she have any inkling that this disastrous day was by no means over . . .

CHAPTER FOUR

SHE was about half way home when the car faltered and spluttered, accepted her worried dictates that steered it off the road, and there the motor died with an apologetic cough. Hannah stared at the petrol gauge with her heart suddenly in her mouth, and immediately knew why it had stopped. She'd been going to fill it up that morning, but in all the drama, had totally forgotten about it.

What was worse, though, was that she was stranded on a deserted part of the back road from Broadbeach to Nerang and even if she did manage to flag down a passing motorist to drive her to the nearest service station and back, she had no money with her—not a cent.

'Oh no,' she groaned and leant her head tiredly against the steering wheel. 'What do I do now? I suppose I could start to walk, but it's a good couple of miles to the nearest house where I might be able to ring up from and then . . .'

She groaned again as she thought that if this day ran true to form, she was bound to get hold of Alex, and the thought of explaining yet another silly predicament to him was more than she could bear.

Then she jumped at an ominous sound and twisted round to peer out of the back window to see that huge, boiling black clouds had rolled in from the sea, presaging, if she was any judge, quite a storm. She closed her eyes and sat back wearily, feeling helpless and hopeless and as if she had the weight of the world pressing down on her slim shoulders.

She sat like that for some time, listening to the thunder, then she opened the door and stepped out and jumped as a passing car flashed past her to come to a squealing halt and then reverse back towards her . . .

It was a Mercedes coupé, one that she'd seen before, and before her incredulous eyes, it stopped level with her and Matt Bartholomew stepped out.

'Hannah,' he said with a grin. 'Fancy finding you here! What's gone wrong?'

'I . . . I've run out of petrol,' she said despairingly then brightened a fraction. 'You don't . . . you wouldn't happen to carry a petrol tin—and a piece of hose, so that I could milk just a little from your tank? Enough to get me home? I'd repay you . . .'

He looked at her amusedly. 'I'm afraid not. There's no problem, I can drive you home.'

She frowned faintly. 'Oh, I couldn't ask you to do that. You're going in the opposite direction for one thing. If you could perhaps . . . Well, if I could phone from somewhere!' She had to raise her voice as a gust of wind rattled the grass and the first drops of rain began to fall.

'Hannah,' he said, 'this is quite a storm coming up. You don't want to be out in it. I'm afraid you're going to have to accept my lift home whether you like it or not . . .'

'But what about the car?'

'One thing's for sure—no one could drive it away and it's off the road . . . Has someone warned you recently about accepting lifts from strange men? I'm not a stranger, am I?'

'No, no,' Hannah said hastily. 'I mean . . .'

He studied her, then smiled faintly. 'Then someone's been warning you about *me*, and you imagine I'm going to abduct you and carry you off to my castle, to a fate worse than death?' he said patiently, although it was now raining quite heavily and the wind was getting ever stronger.

'I don't imagine anything of the kind,' Hannah said crossly. Cross mainly, she realised, because if no one had ever mentioned anything about Matt Bartholomew she might not be standing in the middle of the road making a fool of herself. His words had exactly captured the kind of vague fears she'd had about him, but at the same time made them seen quite ludicrous.

She bit her lip, coloured and felt extremely foolish—even more so when he said, 'We're getting wet, Hannah . . .'

'Oh. Yes, well—thank you very much. I guess it is the best thing to do.'

'Not at all,' he said suavely, but with the same kind of amusement in his eyes Alex sometimes surveyed her with—used to, rather, she amended and climbed in the Mercedes.

'By the way, your boss was looking for you earlier,' Matt Bartholomew murmured as he set the car in motion and swung it round in the opposite direction.

Hannah glanced at him nervously.

'Yes,' he said, taking his eyes off the road to smile at her. 'I . . . uh . . . got the impression you'd gone AWOL, but I could be wrong.'

'Gone . . .?'

'Away without leave. At least, Alex wasn't in a very good mood at the same time he was looking for you.'

Hannah digested this in silence and didn't quite manage to suppress a shiver.

'Have you two had a tiff?' Matt Bartholomew asked casually.

'I . . . you could say so, I guess,' Hannah murmured.

'Want to tell me about it? Hell,' he added as the heavens opened and the rain fell down like a solid sheet of water reducing his visibility to almost nil in the growing, storm-laden dusk.

'N-no, thank you very much,' Hannah said in a small voice. 'It was mostly my fault anyway . . .' Her voice tailed off and to her horror she felt two large tears tremble on her eyelashes and trickle down her cheeks.

'My dear child,' Matt Bartholomew said and pulled the car off the road.

Hannah stiffened and turned to him urgently. 'What are you doing?'

'I can't drive in this,' he said, with a flicker of a smile. 'It's only inviting an accident, but it will pass quickly enough, these violent storms usually do. Besides we're only about a mile away now and you can get all your problems off your chest in the meantime. It nearly always helps to talk to someone and I'm a very reliable confidant, you know. Has he been a brute to you? He can be sometimes.'

Hannah moved uncomfortably in her seat and began to wish the subject had never come up. 'No,' she said and strove for a light tone that would belie her tears. 'I got myself into a very awkward situation this morning which he . . . he had to help me get out of . . .'

'Tell me about it,' he prompted.

She did, reluctantly, but not the sequel that had occurred in Alex's study and Matt Bartholomew grinned sympathetically and, unbeknownst to her, restrained himself from laughing heartily.

He said, 'I don't see the problem. It could have happened to anyone.'

She turned to him almost eagerly. 'That's what I said! Oh, but I have to admit these things happen to me all the time. I do think I'm a bit of a trial to . . . to people.' She sighed heavily. 'In fact I've sometimes thought of becoming a nun. I sometimes think that's all that might be left to me,' she added humorously, 'because one thing I could do, is teach the Gospel from memory, but I suppose nuns need to be above the kind of scrapes I get into.'

She said all this half laughingly, and with not much sincerity, because in her entire life she'd never been able to picture herself as a nun. A minister maybe, free to roam the outback ... Then she realised she was only talking this way out of a mixture of nerves and an almost feverish impatience to get out of the storm and enlist someone's aid—Marge's probably—to get her car back to the property without Alex knowing that she'd run out of petrol on top of everything else.

As she grimaced and looked at her tall, red-headed companion in anticipation of a similar sense of humour, she got the shock of her life because he wasn't laughing or reciprocating her small nervous flight into fancy at all. He was looking at her with a deadly intentness instead, a look that she recognised instantly because she'd seen it before, although it was usually cloaked with a grin. There was no mistaking it now, however, and she sucked in a breath and tensed visibly.

'I . . .'

His arm slid around her shoulder. 'You what?' he asked, his lips barely moving. 'Do you know you have the most adorable, most un-nun-like mouth I've ever seen, Hannah? It would be a crying shame to see you locked up in a convent, because you were made to be loved and kissed.'

'I wasn't serious,' she whispered and blushed immediately as she realised how ambiguous her words had sounded.

'Do that again,' he murmured. 'I adore it. In fact to see you blush has the most devastating effect on me. What's more, I've put a lid on it for *weeks*, but I can't resist a moment longer.' And he lowered his head and sought her lips with his.

Hannah was never sure afterwards what it was that moved her to panic the way she did. Even at the time, she thought to herself that there had to be another way to handle this. Her thoughts deserted her at that point, and left her in the grip of a mindless, blazing panic that saw her deliver the same treatment she had, weeks ago, to Billy Johnson. She twisted her head away and delivered a resounding blow to Matt Bartholomew's cheek and was horrified to see that far from deterring him, it seemed actually to add to his enjoyment and sense of anticipation.

'Why you little wildcat!' he growled low in his throat. 'You'll pay for that and love every minute of it. Is that why you did it?'

'No!' she sobbed. '*No*. Will you . . . let me go,' she panted, twisting and turning in his arms, desperately. 'Let me go!'

'Not just yet, sweetheart,' he drawled and snaked a hand through her hair. 'By God you've got some spirit and I like that.' His lips descended on hers again and forced them apart and his tongue plundered her mouth, while his hand remained in her hair so that every evasive movement she made, brought her a red-hot, eye-watering sensation of pain.

That would have been the time to desist, she'd thought later. That should have been when she'd gone limp and projected an image of sheer disgust—but passively. At the time, though, while she'd felt the disgust vividly, she'd found it impossible to submit to the indignity of it with anything that could have been taken for acquiescence. Besides, it wasn't only disgust that flowed through her veins in a living tide but a flame of fury too.

She wrenched her mouth free, finally, and cried, 'Oh, they were so right about you! Billy Johnson is worth ten of you,' she added a little irrationally but furiously.

For a moment his hold on her relaxed slightly and he said incredulously, 'Billy Johnson?'

'*Yes.*'

He laughed. 'I thought it was Alex—in fact I was pretty sure it was. As a matter of fact he warned me off you, as if you were his daughter. I should warn you, sweetheart, Alex Cameron hasn't got a heart. He lost it years ago and in its place there's a solid block of marble. As for Billy, he'd be like an under-sized orang-utan trying to play a violin, as the saying goes. That's how he'd make love to you, so I'd forget him.'

Hannah stared up at him with utter loathing and contempt in her eyes, but he only laughed and tightened his arms around her.

There followed a violent couple of minutes during which Hannah bit and scratched and fought with about as much success as a terrified rabbit.

Then there was a sickening and unexpected bang that jolted them both forward and caused Matt Bartholomew to raise his head and swear viciously and fluently. 'Someone's run into the back of us . . .'

To her dying day, Hannah could remember thinking—the Lord does work in mysterious ways!

She took full advantage of this intervention, in a manner that gave credit to her reflexes. She had her door open in a flash and she slipped out of the car like an eel, despite his thunderous imprecation and out-thrust hand. Then she was running through the rain with the sound of a strange, but equally angry voice, calling down the wrath of God on, she hoped devoutly, Matt Bartholomew.

'Only a mile,' she panted to herself as she forced herself to keep on going despite aching legs and the driving rain and bursting lungs. 'It . . . can't be much further. Oh God! He could overtake me so easily in the car. Please make sure he can't get mobile again until I get home . . .'

Then with a sob of relief, she saw the white gateposts with their lighted lamps on top, swim up out of the rain and she was just passing through when she was forced to stop and double up because of a stitch in her side, and she didn't realise a car was coming down the driveway towards her until she looked up and was dazzled by the headlights and heard the screech of its tyres as it stopped only inches from her.

Through the mist of pain that had her in its grip, and the teeming rain that had reduced her to a sodden, muddy mess, she knew it would have to be Alex to find her like this. She knew it with a morbid certainty even before his tall figure loomed over her and he said her name in a way that left her in no doubt as to his state of mind.

And she found all she was capable of was sinking to the wet tarmac with her face in her hands.

'Now,' her employer said to her grimly, 'would you like to explain yourself?'

Hannah looked hopelessly down at the glass of brandy in her hands and could think of no way to begin even. Yet this moment had hung over her head like a Sword of Damocles for the past hour. Ever since Alex had scooped her up off the driveway in fact, and through all that had followed—Mrs Hunter's vocal surprise at being presented with Hannah and told to clean her up. Which she'd done per medium of a bath and some dry clothing, which she'd provided herself temporarily, until the rain stopped. She'd clicked her tongue amazedly several times as she'd applied a bright red antiseptic to the impressive array of grazes and scrapes Hannah had acquired from a variety of sources, but mostly from slipping on the wet road a couple of times.

'And you're bruised!' she had said incredulously. 'On your neck and shoulders almost as if you've been . . . but of course it couldn't be that . . .'

Hannah had looked at herself in the mirror for the first time and shuddered. Then she'd said quietly, 'Please don't put any more of that stuff on me. I look like a patchwork quilt as it is.'

'What you really need is a cold compress for the bruises—what did happen to you, love?'

Hannah had been saved from that set of explanations by the arrival of Alex in the adjoining bedroom. He'd brought two brandies with him and dispensed with Mrs Hunter's services quite bluntly, much to that lady's chagrin, and he had told Hannah curtly to sit down.

She'd looked around at what was a guest bedroom and had said uncertainly, 'Here?'

'Yes, here,' he'd said sardonically, his gaze flickering over her battered person clad in a large pair of Mrs Hunter's floral cotton pyjamas and then he'd looked into her eyes so implacably, she'd sunk down into one of the two chintz-covered armchairs.

Where she still sat, nursing her brandy.

'I'm waiting, Hannah.'

The words were quiet enough, but there was no mistaking the menace behind them and she took a gulp

of brandy to steady her nerves. 'I . . . I did something
stupid,' she said lamely, and bit her lip, only to wince
with pain.

'You surprise me,' Alex Cameron said mockingly.

He was standing near the window and he'd changed
too, into a pair of light trousers and a dark brown
cotton knit top. His thick dark hair was still damp and
she thought he looked terrifyingly tall and unbelievably
attractive, even although his mouth was set in a hard
line as he stared down at the drink in his hand, waiting
for her to go on.

Then his eyelashes lifted suddenly and his dark eyes
that she'd so mistakenly thought sleepy, bored into her
own and she felt her cheeks go red and her mind reel
with confusion. How could I—when I often hate him
and am sometimes scared of him—how could I
basically still feel the same about him? How can it be
like a slow form of torture to be near him and have to
hide it, *try* to hide it after the things he said to me this
morning? Am I hiding it, though? Perhaps not, if Matt
Bartholomew could work it out . . .

Oh God, she thought and tore her gaze away. Is this
some sort of poetic justice. When I think of how
superior I was about Billy . . .

'Hannah.' His voice interrupted her tortured
thoughts. 'Look at me.'

She swallowed and forced herself to look up.

'Now,' he said, very quietly and deliberately, 'will
you tell me how it comes that you look like a cross
between an accident and a rape victim? Just start at
the beginning which, from what I gather, is some time
after you left the Claytons.'

Her eyes widened. 'How did you know that?'

'Because,' he said shortly, 'when you chose to
disappear all day, it occurred to me finally, that's

where you might have gone. I'd just rung them before I nearly ran over you in the driveway. They said you'd left some time ago and should have beaten the storm home. You hadn't, though, so I was going out to find you.'

'I . . . I was in an accident,' she said unhappily and wondered again, which was the more awkward aspect of it all. The fact that she'd got herself into another scrape or Matt Bartholomew's part in it. After all he was a friend and a partner.

'Where's the car?' Alex asked tersely.

'Oh, not in your car!' she said quickly and stopped abruptly.

'Go on, Hannah.'

She took a deep breath and realising she had no choice, told him almost everything and when she'd finished there was a tense silence until he said almost idly, 'You accepted a lift from a stranger? I should have thought even you would have known better.'

'He wasn't . . . I mean, well, I didn't know what else to do!'

'You could have walked to the nearest house and asked them to ring me.'

'The nearest house wasn't that near,' she said defiantly, 'and it was about to pour. Besides,' she added candidly, for a moment unreasonably cross, 'after what you said to me this morning, that was the last thing I felt like doing. Look,' she put her drink down and stood up, 'I'm tired and I've still got to get your car back—somehow. Can't we dispense with all this? If it makes you feel any better, I stand convicted on all counts. I'm an idiot, but although I got myself into it, I also got myself out of it. With some help from the Lord above . . .' she added a little lamely.

His eyes glinted with a look of pure anger as he

straightened and walked towards her so that she
stepped backwards and sat down again unexpectedly.

'You're going nowhere, Hannah and it's not that
simple,' he said in a voice loaded with contempt.

'W-what do you mean,' she stammered, and only by
a great effort of will, stopped herself from shrinking
back into the chair.

He stared down at her, with his mouth compressed
into a rigid white line and his eyes going over her
swollen bottom lip where she'd bitten it herself in
fright. Then he seemed to relax deliberately and he
pulled the other chair round and sat down opposite
her.

'For one thing, you say—with some pride—that you
got yourself out of it, but another girl might not be so
lucky one day. Which means, to my mind, that we
have no choice but to inform the police. You must be
able to remember the make of the car at least and some
details of your . . . assailant.'

Hannah's mouth dropped open. 'Oh, but . . .' she
said awkwardly. 'I mean—what I mean is, I think I
might have been partly responsible for it.'

Alex's eyebrows shot up. 'How?'

'Well,' she swallowed, 'I don't *think* he meant to do
any more than kiss me, but I . . . panicked,' she said
miserably.

He looked at her expressionlessly for what seemed
like a long time. Then he said, 'Does that mean you
think any strange man has the right to kiss you?'

'No, of course not, but . . .'

He waited for her to finish and when she didn't he
said, 'And what form of ESP gave you the idea that all
he wanted to do was kiss you even while you panicked
to the extent that you did?'

'I don't know,' she said desperately and jumped up

but he was on his feet almost as quickly to clamp a
hand around her upper arm.

'Tell me, Hannah,' he threatened. 'You see there's
something I don't quite grasp about this. Why are you
trying to protect the person who did this to you?' He
traced his finger down her jawline so that she winced
as it passed over a bruise that was visibly starting to
darken.

'It's not that,' she cried, suddenly near the end of
her tether. 'Not the way you think it is, anyway, but
... but ...'

A sudden light of comprehension dawned in his eyes
and he interrupted her harshly. 'It was someone you
knew, wasn't it?'

'Oh ... yes,' she said distraughtly and shivered as
he lifted his gaze to stare across her head unseeingly,
but as if he was mentally reviewing something.

Then he said, 'Not ... Matt Bartholomew?' And
when she tensed, he added, 'I might have known.
You're a bigger fool than I thought you were, Hannah.
Didn't you know he's been eyeing you for weeks?'

'I ... oh,' she said wretchedly, 'I didn't know what
to think. I didn't know what to *do*.' She started to
shake. 'I was in such a jam, you see. And ... and if
you hadn't been so horrible to me this morning I
might not have been in that jam in the first place.
I might not have said what I did, which probably started him off ... about becoming a nun ...'
Tears of utter misery and confusion gathered in her
eyes.

'Becoming a nun?' he said and laughed, but it
wasn't with particular humour. 'It's my fault now, is
it?' he added and the very contained way he said it
made her catch her breath in sudden fright. He went
on, 'Then we'll have to do something about that,

won't we? We'll have to make sure you don't get in to any more of these jams on account of other people and *not* because you don't have the faintest idea how to look after yourself,' he drawled, his eyes suddenly lazy and mocking. 'For old times' sake at least, because I'd hate to have you on my conscience, Hannah. Once you get used to the idea, you might find it's not so . . . strange to you, after all.'

'I . . . I don't have the faintest idea what you're talking about,' she whispered.

'Don't you?' he queried and slid his arms around her. 'I wonder . . .' He smiled, a slight, cool twisting of his lips. 'I'm talking about us getting married, my dear. At least then I'll be able to protect you from yourself and the big bad world out there that you find so hard to handle. You'll be able to have babies to your heart's content . . .'

'Oh, stop it,' she panted, coming out of her frozen, incredulous dream. 'Don't . . .' Don't do this to me, her heart cried. 'No,' she said distraughtly. 'You can't be serious . . .'

'Why not? Some people say it's as good a reason for getting married as any other,' he observed, with a glitter in his eyes that warned her he was still very angry deep down.

She took a breath and tried to think. 'I'm not one of those people,' she said at last. 'I believe in love.'

He smiled slightly and his hand moved upward to the nape of her neck just gently. 'You might not recognise it if you were hit over the head with it,' he said pensively. 'For example, what did you think it was the night I kissed you in the lemon grove? For you?'

A tide of hot, painful colour rose from the base of Hannah's throat as he looked at her searchingly, she dropped her gaze and tried to free herself with clumsy, uncoordinated movements.

He resisted them easily enough. 'Look at me, Hannah.'

'No, I can't,' she answered in a suffocated voice. 'And I can't marry you either. Th-thank you all the same, but I just can't.'

'*All* the same you will, my dear,' he murmured.

'Alex,' she breathed despairingly and began to cry and shiver, hot helpless tears she couldn't control any more than she could stop her body from shaking with reaction and emotion . . .

He brought his hands up very slowly to cup her face and smudge her tears with his fingers. Then she found herself leaning against him, crying into his shoulder and trying at the same time to apologise for being such a fool, and getting the hiccups. But as he simply held her close, a feeling of . . . safety, she thought dimly, and warmth, began to creep over her so that finally, she was still and she looked up at him with her eyes wide and still tear-drenched and a little wondering. Then, with a strangely husky sound, she let herself relax completely . . .

'Hannah Rosemary . . .'

Hannah turned her head and blinked, and realised it was she who'd been saying her name slowly and dreamily as she swam up out of a deep sleep.

The room was full of sunlight and the curtains billowed as a breeze wafted in, to bring with it the mingled perfume of orange blossom and damp earth, and she lay quite still and knew that the ground outside would be steaming slightly in the bright, hot sunshine after the drenching of last night.

Then she wondered what time it was and thought it

might be quite late, later than she normally got up.
She wondered, too, why she felt so ... it was hard to
describe, but mixed with a sort of soothing feeling of
lassitude there was a slight ache in her lower back. She
remembered suddenly that she'd awoken with her
name on her lips and she frowned faintly and suddenly
jerked upright as she realised what she'd been
dreaming, and what she'd been saying ... Hannah
Rosemary, do you take this man to be ...

The events of the previous evening tumbled vividly
into place and she went hot and cold as she thought,
Oh God! What have I done? *Oh* ...

She lay back, with her mind in an incredible turmoil
and her cheeks flushed and her hands trembling as she
recalled how she'd given herself to Alex—not once,
but twice ...

The first time had been a mindless sort of thing on
her part, a thing of curious sensations as his hands had
roamed her body at will, very gently. And she'd talked
to him all the time, still trying to explain that she
didn't mean to be a burden to anyone. Finally,
however, he'd put a finger on her lips and she'd found
herself kissing his hand and then very shyly putting
her arms around his neck and then hugging him with a
curious intensity because she knew she ought not to be
yet it was as if her stunned, dazed mind could no more
turn away from this warmth and contact that only
Alex could make so special for her, than she could fly.

So it had happened. The very thing she'd thought
she was immune to and Marge, and Alex himself,
ironically, had worried about happening to her. She'd
cried a little because although he'd been incredibly
gentle, it had hurt fleetingly, but her tears had had no
regret in them ...

The second time had been just before dawn when

she'd woken with a sense of panic in her heart because she hadn't known where she was. Alex had stirred beside her and murmured her name and taken her in his arms and it had happened again, that blending of bodies that made her feel as if she'd never be lonely again, the kind of closeness she'd wondered about without really knowing how it could be. And it hadn't hurt at all and she'd fallen asleep again in his arms.

He wasn't there now though, and without his presence she felt suddenly afraid and confused, with all sorts of thoughts creeping up on her . . . Did I get— seduced? No, no, *Alex* wouldn't do that to me and anyway I let him, I wanted him to . . . but . . .

Until finally she whispered to herself, 'But how could I marry him? He can't *really* want to marry me. Only to . . . oh, God!'

'Oh, there you are, Hannah,' Mrs Hunter said as Hannah came downstairs slowly. 'Alex said to let you sleep a bit but I kept some breakfast for you. Well, you do look better, love, I must say,' she added with her head cocked to one side. 'It's amazing what a good sleep can do!'

Hannah looked away with her heart beating uncomfortably because incredibly, it appeared that Mrs Hunter did not know what had transpired last night. She said awkwardly, 'I don't feel like breakfast, thank you very much, Mrs Hunter.'

'A cup of coffee then,' Mrs Hunter suggested. 'I'm not a breakfast person myself. Tell you what, you can take it into the study with you. Alex wants to see you, he said.'

Hannah swallowed and clenched her fists.

The study windows were wide open and the view from them already beginning to shimmer in a heat haze.

Alex lifted his head and surveyed her standing uncertainly in the doorway with a steaming cup of coffee in her hands. A slow smile crept into his eyes at the colour that poured into her face. Awful confusion made her look away helplessly and wonder how she could feel so shy and nervous and God knows what, after last night.

He stood up leisurely and came round the desk to rescue the cup from her suddenly nerveless fingers. 'Good morning, Mrs Cameron-to-be,' he said idly and bent his head to kiss her lightly on the lips. 'You look a lot better this morning.'

She took an urgent breath. 'Alex . . .'

He raised his eyebrows enquiringly, but there was a gleam of laughter in those dark eyes and she got the oddest feeling that he knew exactly what she'd come to say, and that it would be quite futile to say it.

I have to do it, though, she thought with despair. I have to make him see reason . . . She squared her shoulders and moved away from him resolutely.

'I can't marry you, Alex,' she said stiffly. 'And I think it's best if I just go away now.'

'Best for whom?' he asked after a moment.

She frowned and warned herself to concentrate. Surely he must see it was best for him?

'Best for both of us. Look,' she swung round and faced him earnestly, 'I've been thinking since I woke up. You told me once you had a terrible temper. I think it must be the same kind of thing my father suffered from—something other people can't *see*. I think, deep down, you were very angry with me last night because I'm such a trial to you. My father also used to say that when one is in the grip of a cold rage like that, you do things you often can't understand later . . .'

Her articulateness deserted her for a moment at that
point, as she saw him studying her thoughtfully, as if
something full of irony had occurred to him, but all he
said was, 'Go on.'

She bit her lip. 'And, well, no one knows, do they?
Mrs Hunter doesn't seem to and she's the only person
who could and I'll eat my hat if she does,' she said
frankly. 'She doesn't strike me as at all the kind of
person who would have greeted me so cheerfully this
morning if she'd known that ... known ...' She
floundered miserably.

His lips twitched. 'When Mrs Hunter retires to her
room and her beloved telly, the house could burn
down around her. Especially if she feels she's not
wanted, which she probably did last night.'

'Well, then,' Hannah rubbed her hands together,
'unless ... but I don't think ...' She tailed off
disjointedly.

'You think there might be other signs for her to
detect?' he offered gravely. 'I shouldn't worry about it.
You have quite an impressive array of gashes and
grazes to account for that. I hope I didn't add to your
... to that sort of discomfort last night,' he added
suddenly serious.

Hannah stared at him bewilderedly.

'I meant,' he said then, a little wryly, 'that when
you're a virgin ...' He stopped as she blushed, and he
touched her hot cheek lightly and fondly.

Hannah, who had forgotten her grazes and bruises
in the over-all enormity of her recent experiences,
said, uncomfortably, 'Oh. That ... I guess you're
right.' Then, 'No, I've fallen off too many horses to be
worried by a few scrapes.' She grimaced. 'But I didn't
think of that. I wondered ... oh, it doesn't matter.'

'Tell me.'

'Well—I think it probably sounds silly so I won't say it.' She smiled feebly, but her smile faded as she saw he was still waiting, with his eyebrows raised quizzically. She sighed. 'I looked at myself in the mirror this morning—to see if I looked any different. I thought I must because I felt ... I mean ...' She shrugged, embarrassed.

'You wondered if it would show outwardly that you were now a woman?' he supplied, with a faintly whimsical note in his voice and an odd smile touching his lips.

'It *does* sound silly. I thought it might,' she said with resignation. 'Don't you see, that would be another problem for us. Technically I might be a woman but actually I'm still only—I mean you think of me, really, as ...'

'Hannah,' he interrupted, with that whimsy replaced by a sort of harsh compassion that was tinged with impatience, 'let's not get technical about this. You are a woman now and you became one because of me—you didn't have any choice and we're going to get married.'

'But I did have a choice!' she cried. 'I ... it wasn't as if you used force or anything like that. I ... oh,' she whispered, and felt tears welling up.

He took her hand and kissed her palm then folded her fingers over it. 'That ... you wanted what happened last night,' he said as if choosing his words with care, 'is a very good reason for us to get married, Hannah, one of the best in fact.'

There was silence and the tears overflowed and spilled down her face until she said finally and unhappily, 'I did ... I have wondered about you—like that. But it could ... well, girls go through that kind of thing, don't they? And ...'

'Not only girls.'

'I mean—when you're young, you . . . But,' she said unsteadily, 'up until last night *you* never showed any sign of—that I wasn't just a troublesome child, so *I* know you only want to marry me because . . . because of what happened in the heat of the moment, which I didn't exactly help, and because of a debt you feel you might owe my father.' She stared up at him with her lips white and set.

She was totally taken aback when he said on a note of almost detached interest, 'Would you believe me if I told you I loved you, Hannah?'

'I . . . no!' she said indignantly at last. 'That's what I'm trying to say!'

'Then,' he looked at her consideringly, 'do you think we could learn to love each other?'

Her lips parted and his dark eyes captured hers and it was as if he could see right into her soul, to that secret she was so afraid she might have given away last night . . .

She wrenched her gaze away and said confusedly, 'I don't know. How would that help, though, if I could and you couldn't . . . or the other way around?' As if it's likely to be that way around, her heart taunted her. As if it hasn't happened the other way around already!

'Who's to say *we* couldn't. We . . . got off to a good start last night.'

'No,' she said, the tears falling faster now. 'No . . .'

'Hannah.' She felt his fingers on her face so that she was forced to look up. 'I'm surprised at you,' he said very gently. 'I thought you could never resist a challenge. After last night, I thought you might not mind us learning to love each other. After all, it cuts both ways, doesn't it?'

'H-how?'

'Well, you've said you think you're a great trial to me, but you must admit I often make you very cross.'

'. . . Yes, but I don't see . . .'

'Perhaps we could learn from each other. You have qualities I admire very much.'

'I do?' she said doubtfully.

He smiled faintly. 'Yes. Not the least of which is your painful honesty. By the way, when you learn a bit more, Hannah, you'll understand that you didn't have any choice last night. So don't torment yourself about that.'

It took her a long time to marshal her thoughts. To say finally in a husky voice, 'But I have a choice now, don't I?'

'No.'

'Yes,' she whispered, despairingly.

'No.' He traced the outline of her mouth with its still swollen bottom lip. 'Do you really think I would—do what I did, to you of all people, and then stand back as if it had never happened?' he said, on a curiously rough note.

'I . . .'

'Well you're mistaken, Hannah,' he said coolly. 'And there's something else you might not have taken into calculation—you could be pregnant.'

She tensed violently and a shadow of a smile crept into his eyes.

She licked her lips. 'I did think of that,' she admitted and swallowed painfully. 'But I should imagine that, statistically, it's probably very unlikely.'

His smile deepened into a grin and his eyes gleamed with little points of sheer devilry as he said, 'I'm told that's one of the most fallible statistics known to man.' He added idly, 'And, as you once remarked to me about statistics in general and lifts in particular, it's all very well to console yourself with them but they're not much help to you when you crash to the bottom of the shaft.' He sobered suddenly and said quietly, 'Hannah, despite what you might like to believe, I shall be honoured to marry you, and I shall look forward to our children too.'

She stared at him wordlessly.

CHAPTER FIVE

THEY were married ten days later.

It was a private ceremony because, as Alex had said, with a grin, it would be far simpler to present everyone with a *fait accompli*. Hannah had found herself in complete agreement with this.

It was the Reverend Clayton who married them despite Hannah's nervous dread of how they were going to explain it to him.

It was Alex, however, who had made the explanations. He'd said simply that he and Hannah had come to care very greatly for each other and wanted to get married. He'd said too, as Hannah's hand had trembled in his, that there seemed no reason to delay the wedding, since they'd known each other for six months now.

The Reverend Ted had looked startled and bewildered but when he had turned to Hannah for confirmation, she had coloured delicately, yet said, 'I know this must be a surprise for you, but, well, it's what I want too.'

All the same he'd persuaded Alex to leave Hannah at the Rectory while he went into the office so that she could wait for Mrs Clayton who was out, to tell her the news personally.

'Now, Hannah,' he said, when Alex had left with an unseen, final and reassuring pressure on Hannah's fingers. 'I must admit you've almost floored me! Are you . . . are you very sure about this?'

'Yes,' Hannah said with a calmness that surprised

her. Perhaps it wasn't so surprising though, because
over the last two days she had argued everything out
with herself—it felt like ten thousand times—and had
come up with some surprising answers. For example,
the discovery that a delicate little tendril of hope had
sprung up in her heart. The hope that she might one
day make Alex forget Alison Fairleigh ... Then there
was the question of being pregnant. She had no idea
how soon one could find out about it, outside the
natural course of events, but somehow, the thought of
basing a decision to get married on the outcome of a
test, seemed wrong to her. Wouldn't it be rather like
making the child a scapegoat to say—I won't agree to
marry you now but I will if there's to be a baby? she
asked herself. Could you ever feel right about that?

Of course, there were the not so surprising aspects
of it too. The fact that she loved Alex and that nothing
seemed to change it. The bottom line of it all seemed
to be that he wasn't going to give her any choice and
short of running away, what was she to do? She'd
thought of telling the Claytons what had happened,
but had discarded the idea because she knew without
being told, in what light Alex would immediately
appear to them, and she doubted very much that she
would be able to make them see that she had been as
much responsible ...

And through all of her arguments with herself, there
was the curiously shaking thought, that she could
never regret what had happened ... She wondered if
this was brazen of her, or foolhardy, or both, but
discovered it didn't seem to matter.

Nor, this morning when Alex had suggested coming
to see the Reverend Ted, had she said any of the
things that she should have said—repeated any of the
arguments against this marriage. Instead she'd looked

at him and felt her heart move in her breast, and agreed.

She discovered that, apart from her uncertainty about how their news was going to be received, she felt as if she had been relieved of a great weight . . .

'My dear, forgive me,' Ted Clayton said, 'but I look upon you very much as the daughter I never had. So I feel we ought to have a talk about this. Sometimes our senses betray us into mistaking a physical attraction for love. Have you thought about that?'

Hannah considered. Then she said, 'But you can't separate the two either, can you? I've also had months now to find out that . . . well, sometimes Alex makes me mad, sometimes sad, but nothing he ever does makes me not trust him or not want to be with him. I . . . I love him very much,' she said very quietly.

'He—he's quite a bit older than you, Hannah.'

'I know. I think that'll be good for me. I don't get on very well with young men. Don't you like him?' she asked, with suddenly anxious eyes.

'As a matter of fact, I do. But I feel I have to point out to you that marriage is never a bed of roses and because of the age difference—well, that could make it harder.'

Hannah winced inwardly, but she said steadily, 'I know that there will be times when it probably won't be easy for either of us. Sometimes I'm . . . a great trial to everyone.' She looked rueful. 'Alex is like . . . I don't know how to say it. He . . . reassures me. I feel safe with him.'

'Hannah,' Ted Clayton hesitated and then was surprised to hear himself say, 'don't sell yourself short. If you love him as you seem to, then be proud of it. Two people who love each other have to be equals in that respect. Are you a little worried,' he said

acutely, 'that you may be—how can I put it, not quite
up to him in some respects?'

Hannah stared at her hands for a long time. 'Just
sometimes,' she admitted finally, and added, 'I think I
might have to grow up quite quickly in some respects,
but I also know that I *could* say I was too young for
this, and spend the rest of my life regretting it.'

Ted Clayton was silent. Then he said, 'If you're
very sure of that.'

'I am,' Hannah answered.

'Then you have my blessing, my dear.'

Alex looked at Hannah rather searchingly when he
came to pick her up.

'I didn't change my mind,' she said when they were
in the car.

'Did he try to make you?'

'No . . .'

'All the same, though, you feel as if you're deceiving
him?' he asked perceptively.

Hannah was silent.

Alex picked up her hand and held it on the steering
wheel with his. 'Trust me, Hannah,' he said.

'All the same, I just don't know . . .'

'Don't know what, dear?' Mrs Clayton said drowsily
and then sat up resignedly and reached out to switch
on the bedside lamp. Years of experience had taught
her that when her husband carried on a conversation
with himself in the middle of the night, it was no use
adjuring him to go back to sleep, and it was impossible to
sleep *through* it, until he had got it all off his chest.

'I just don't know about Alex Cameron,' Ted
Clayton said. 'I mean, I quite like the man, but . . .'
He shrugged.

'You once told me you liked him very much,' Mrs Clayton remarked.

'That was before I knew he was going to want to marry Hannah,' her husband replied with a touch of irritability.

'I don't see what difference that makes. You surely wouldn't want Hannah to marry someone you didn't like.'

'Of course I wouldn't!' Ted Clayton cast his wife a look of ruffled impatience. 'I just don't know if he's the right one for her!'

'Because he's older?' Mrs Clayton enquired. 'If you ask me, I think that's just what Hannah needs.'

'So does Hannah!'

'There is no need to make me the target of your sarcasm, Ted,' Mrs Clayton said serenely and added obscurely, 'All fathers have the same problem.'

'I am not . . .'

'I think you consider yourself one albeit by proxy. It's a well known fact that fathers very often don't think *anyone* is good enough for their daughters.'

'I would never have got into this conversation with you if I'd known you were going to be trite.'

'Me? In the middle of the night? Why, Ted!' Mrs Clayton chuckled. 'Never mind. I'll let you go back to sleep again . . .' She turned over.

'Don't you dare,' Ted Clayton said, with a rueful grin. 'I'm sorry . . . but I can't help being concerned. I mean, it came as such a surprise for one thing!'

'Well, not to me, I must confess, Ted.'

Ted Clayton turned to her incredulously. 'Did Hannah tell you?'

'No. But there are some things one can . . . discern from a person's conversation.'

'I didn't!'

Mrs Clayton was silent.

'All right,' her husband said at last. 'Don't say it! I suppose I am an unobservant mere male. So,' he added on a more serious note, 'you're not ... as concerned as I obviously am about this marriage?'

Mrs Clayton took her time about replying. 'Ted,' she said finally, 'no one can really know how it is between a man and a woman, so I can't say with any certainty that this marriage is ideal. Only time will tell that. But I like and respect Alex Cameron and I have this feeling that Hannah is in good hands. Which is something of a relief to me, I must admit. It's not that I doubt her morals or her integrity in the slightest. In fact it's a bit because of them—now don't ask me to explain that because I can't! It's just something I feel. Hannah is ... well, vulnerable to her conscience, you see. More so than most. Therefore, I'm in fact happy about this marriage. She needs an anchor.'

Ted Clayton thought for a long time. 'And you think he's the right one?'

'I think *he* must think he is otherwise he wouldn't be marrying her. He's not a fool or a boy.'

'Do you think ... I mean, do you remember when we were first in love? Do you think it's the same for them? For that matter, how we often still are after all these years ...?'

Mrs Clayton's eyes softened. 'I don't know. She'll be a lucky girl if they are. Of course, I've had a lot to put up with too.' She glanced pointedly at the bedside clock.

'What say I make you a cup of tea now? Would that compensate for some of the things you've had to put up with?'

'Possibly ... just possibly.'

*   *   *

During the days before her wedding, Hannah carried on just as she had before. Mainly because Alex was very busy getting things in order for an unscheduled honeymoon, although Hannah had no idea where they were going.

Nobody seemed to notice anything amiss with her, except Marge, who remarked that she seemed a bit preoccupied. Hannah felt guilty then, because it seemed slightly underhand not to mention anything. On the other hand, the thought of trying to explain the situation appeared monumental.

Because of the rush to get things in order, she found she saw little of Alex, and then it was mostly when she was working with him. Curiously, she was rather glad of this, because it was one thing, she discovered, to make a decision and defend it to herself, but quite another when confronted with her tall, assured husband-to-be, to be *poised* about it. In fact, she alternated between a state of sheer panic at what she'd done and a sense of supreme unreality that this could be happening to Hannah Hawthorn . . .

What was worse, however, was that a lot of her mental turmoil showed through. As on the occasion the day after they'd been to see the Reverend Clayton and they were in Alex's study and he was dictating to her.

He stopped talking and swung his chair round to the window. She waited patiently with her pencil poised, but when he turned back, he said idly. 'I don't suppose you have a passport?'

She blinked. 'Yes I do.'

'Current?'

'Yes. My father was planning to take me to Papua New Guinea just before he died . . . Why do you ask?'

He contemplated her thoughtfully, then smiled

slightly. 'We might as well get it changed to your married name. And I thought we might get ourselves some inoculations over the next couple of days. Would you mind?'

'I . . . no. But why?'

'Well, I thought we might go out of the country for our honeymoon.'

'Where?'

'To be honest, I'm not quite sure. It all depends. So long as you like the idea that's all that matters. Or are you looking upon our wedding as a sort of stepping off the world, Hannah?'

She licked her lips. 'I don't know what you mean.'

'Well you haven't asked any questions about honeymoons or anything about our life together afterwards. In fact you've said nothing to me you wouldn't normally have said . . .'

Hannah blushed suddenly and wondered why it was that she felt totally intimidated by the thought of spending a honeymoon with this man. She cleared her throat and said with an effort, 'I thought we'd probably live a very similar life to what we are now.' She looked at him uncertainly. 'I could still do all this.' She moved a hand to encompass the study. 'I really enjoy it.'

He looked at her lazily then said, 'All right, in lieu of discussing honeymoons, why don't you tell me what you're going to wear to your wedding?'

'I . . .' she stopped, 'hadn't thought of it.' And wondered suddenly what on earth she *was* going to wear.

'Would you like to go shopping this afternoon? For a wedding dress?'

Hannah had an immediate vision of filmy white bridal gowns, and bit her lip. 'No thank you,' she said in some confusion. 'I don't suppose I have to dress up—I mean, really dress up, do I?'

'Not if you don't want to,' he said. 'On the other hand, if you're worried about wearing white, don't be. Because I have no doubt that you're a lot more innocent at heart than many girls who trip to the altar in virginal white.'

She looked away. 'I don't think I could,' she said barely audibly. 'It would be like telling a lie—I think.'

'Then wear your pink dress,' he said after a moment.

She flinched inwardly, but made herself say wryly, 'Definitely a better colour, I agree.'

'Hannah.' He waited until she looked up at him unwillingly. 'That wasn't why I suggested it,' he said steadily. 'I wouldn't be marrying you if I didn't think you had the basic good sense to wear whatever you liked to your wedding, with your head held high.' His dark eyes held hers captive and something she couldn't name flowed between them, some silver thread of communication that inexplicably gave her flagging courage a lift.

She said quietly, 'All right.'

'Good.' His face softened suddenly into a grin and he added teasingly, 'I like you very much in that dress, by the way. *That's* why I suggested it. And you can pack some nightgear and that's all you'll need. By the way, I've got some forms to be signed and I'll need your passport.'

Hannah opened her mouth to speak but the phone rang just then and, by the time he'd finished the call, she'd lost the urge to make any enquiries. He too appeared to only have business on his mind then.

Four days later she was to wonder again, but by that

time she was married and on a plane bound for Perth,
and the memory of her wedding was new in her mind,
but oddly confused. It was a memory of beautiful
flowers in the church, and candlelight and a small
bouquet of white violets for her to carry—Alex's idea,
Mrs Clayton had confided. The service had not been
as she'd feared it would be—hasty and secretive, but
instead solemn and then unexpectedly festive when a
small party of tourists had wandered into the church
and sat as quiet as mice until it was over and then
begged to be allowed to photograph the bride and the
groom and congratulate them and the Claytons on the
beauty of the service and the church and the bride.

Mrs Clayton had added to the celebration by
producing champagne and an exquisitely iced fruit
cake in the Rectory dining room.

It wasn't until they were flying over the Nullabor
that she said, 'Why Perth?'

Alex reached across for her hand, her left hand, with
its shining gold band and delicate engagement ring of
six perfectly matched diamonds set in a curve. 'You'll
see,' he said. 'I never realised you were a nail-biter.'
He looked up, with a smile at the back of his eyes.

'I'm not usually—at least,' she confided wryly, 'I
have done on and off all my life, but I thought I'd
finally got out of it. One day I will.'

'Do you like your ring?'

'Oh yes. I don't know how to thank you . . .' She
looked away in sudden confusion at the glint she saw
in his eyes. 'D-do they know?' she asked in an oddly
breathless voice. 'Everyone at home I mean. Do they
know now?'

'Yes. And they know to expect us back when they
see us. I should imagine the place will be electric at
the moment.'

Yes, Hannah thought.

It was dark by the time they landed in Perth, the
capital of Western Australia, and transferred to a suite
in a luxury hotel. It was then that she suddenly
thought how strange, I've crossed the continent with
only my night things, a change of underwear—and my
new passport. Where can you go from Perth . . .?

But Alex didn't give her time to worry about it. He
rang for a reservation in the restaurant and when she
said hesitantly that she didn't have anything to change
into, he said not to worry, she looked perfect.

Hannah glanced down and found herself laughing a
little.

'What is it?'

She explained. 'When I bought this dress I thought
it might have to see me through day and night and
many special occasions. I had no idea it was going to
be so very true.'

'Oh, we'll take care of the question of clothes
tomorrow,' he said with an answering grin. 'But come,
you must be hungry, you didn't eat anything on the
plane.'

'Yes. Yes, I must be,' she said, but thought hollowly
that she wasn't really because insidiously, the tension
inside her was winding up like an over-loaded spring.

All the same, she managed to hold it at bay for
another two hours and even persuaded herself to eat
something, helped along by the dim atmosphere of the
restaurant and the two glasses of wine she drank. She
even got to the point of scolding herself mentally . . .
After all, you've done it before, Hannah, so why you
should be suffering from wedding night nerves, is a
mystery!

Mystery or not, though, when they were back in the
suite with its muted lighting and fabulous view of the

night skyline of Perth, her flow of small talk dried up like a spring in the desert and she stood in the middle of the lounge twisting her hands uncomfortably.

'What is it?' he said as he came towards her with two glasses of liqueur.

'I ... I don't know,' she stammered, and coloured under his scrutiny as she accepted the glass from him. She took a sip and knew he was still watching her narrowly.

'Please don't think you have to ... I mean ...'

His lips moved in a semblance of a smile. 'Don't you want me to make love to you, Hannah? Is that what you're trying to say?'

No—yes ... I don't know, she thought with despair and lifted her lashes, which were casting absurdly long shadows on her cheeks, to see him turn away to set his glass down and straighten up ...

She took an involuntary step backwards but he didn't move towards her, just took off his tie and shoved his hands deep into his pockets and studied her with a strangely enigmatic expression.

'Tell me, Hannah,' he said at last, in a perfectly casual voice, and to add to her uncertainty, she was suddenly plagued by a disturbingly real vision of his broad, smooth shoulders as if there was no shirt or well-tailored jacket covering them.

'Only if you want to,' she whispered and tried frantically to collect herself. 'I don't know why, but I feel a bit shy,' she said gruffly. 'A little as if this is— unreal, somehow.'

He didn't answer immediately. Then he moved and took her glass and tilted her chin up, in what was becoming a familiar gesture. 'I'm sorry about that,' he murmured. 'Sorry that you should feel it's unreal, but not sorry about the other bit because you're very sweet when you're shy. All the same, we can remedy that. Let's see,' he looked at her gravely, 'tell you what. Come and sit down here.'

He picked her up in his arms and sat down on the settee with her in his lap. 'Comfortable?' he asked, and when she moved her head in a motion that was halfway between a nod and a shake, his lips twitched, but he said in a curiously gentle voice, 'It's always a help to have something to do with your hands at times like these. So, while I undo all these buttons down the front of your dress,' he traced a finger down the line of tiny buttons as he spoke, 'why don't you undo my shirt buttons? After all, this is supposed to be a society based on equality, isn't it?'

She laughed and wasn't sure why and said the first thing that came into her head, 'Japanese women do things like that.'

'So they do,' he commented with a grin. 'They don't seem to have become an endangered species on account of it, either. Maybe they even understand these things better than we do. Why not give it a try?'

'All right,' she said shakily. 'I don't know why I'm making such a fool of myself. I didn't mean to.'

'Perhaps you thought, after the way things happened a few nights ago, and the fact that I haven't really tried to touch you again, until now,' he undid the last button and slid one hand beneath the bodice of her dress to cup her shoulder blade and slide his fingers across her skin, 'that it indicated a lack of interest on my part?' he asked softly.

Hannah trembled at his touch and found she couldn't answer because it was exactly what she had wondered despite the fact that she'd told herself otherwise—that it would be awkward for them both in view of the decision to keep the wedding a secret.

Deep in her heart she'd been unable to suppress the chill thought, that her slightly stunned acceptance of his first lovemaking, and her frightened reaching out for some solace, warmth and comfort and companionship in the bleak hour before dawn, had left him untouched by any burning desire to repeat the experience.

'Hannah.' He trailed his fingers down the side of her neck and round to the delicate skin behind her ear. 'Is that what you thought?'

She moved her head in a tiny motion of assent and tensed as he laughed quietly. 'It wasn't that, you know. I thought you'd prefer it if we did things by the book from then on. Besides, I thought too, it would be good for my...soul,' he said with a touch of dryness, but he didn't explain what he meant when she looked up with puzzled eyes. 'Also, it meant we would have a first for our wedding night because I've never kissed you properly, do you realise? And that's a very special pleasure too. Would you like to try it? I promise you it won't be like ... the way you once experienced it.'

Hannah stared up at him transfixed, her eyes suddenly wide and wary as she recalled Matt Bartholomew's rough, violent invasion of her mouth, and knew suddenly that that was why Alex had kissed her body that night but not her lips.

'I . . .' she said uncertainly, but he silenced her with his firm, cool lips just resting gently on hers and the feel of his fingers sliding through her hair to the nape of her neck. Then he moved his mouth from hers and kissed her eyelids and her throat and the hollows at the base of her neck. The beating of her heart slowed, and she rested for perhaps the first time that day, in some sort of relaxation, soothed by the feel of his lips and his hands. Then her lips parted unconsciously with the pleasure of it and his mouth came down to cover hers.

Later, an age later, it seemed, he lifted his head and stared down at her, to smile faintly at her dazed eyes and she thought, in wonder, that of all the things Alex Cameron had done to her, curiously, this seemed to have been the most intimate—as if they were on equal ground as she'd learnt and followed his lead until everything else, all her fears and uncertainties, had paled from her mind in her absorption of a closer closeness than she'd thought possible.

'Do you want me to make love to you now, Hannah?' His voice was low and deep.

She blinked and found that her voice wasn't working too well, but he saw what was in her eyes and dropped a light kiss on her hair and stood up with her.

The bedroom was dim, illuminated only by the lights outside and a bright moon that turned the terrace tiles beyond the French windows into a sheet of silver. He undressed her slowly and spent a long time caressing her body with his lean strong hands until she was trembling from head to toe. And she brought her hands up, to rest them tentatively on his chest, then to spread her fingers with growing confidence and slide her palms up to his shoulders and round the back of his neck in a shy invitation to him. He accepted, and he kissed her until she felt faint and took her finally in a way that made her feel like an instrument of beauty and pleasure and something more she couldn't name. Finally, he gave her a glimpse of a tantalizing plateau that made her catch her breath because with it came an intimation of almost unbearable delight, should she reach it.

Then their breathing began to subside, and finally

he lay still beside her. She turned to him, touched her lips to his shoulder and fell asleep.

'Africa!' Hannah said incredulously and sat up, only to subside almost immediately and draw up the sheet which her abrupt movement had dislodged.

It was a bright shining day and the sun was pouring on to the terrace from a blue, cloudless sky. She had woken only a few minutes ago, to find she was alone in bed but with the sound of the shower coming from the bathroom.

She had stretched luxuriously and thought of turning over and going to sleep again because she felt oddly lethargic, as if her limbs were drugged with the sensuous feel of nothing but the sheet covering them.

Then the sound of the shower had stopped and Alex had walked into the bedroom wearing only a towel knotted carelessly about his waist and with his head dark and sleek and droplets of water on his shoulders. Hannah had gone still and known her cheeks were pink, but had been unable to do anything about it.

His eyes had teased her as he'd sat down on the side of the bed with an arm on either side of her. Then he'd dropped a light kiss on her head and said wryly, 'You look about fifteen when you're asleep, Hannah. Did you know that? In fact I'm tempted to wonder if I've become a cradle snatcher . . .'

'I don't feel as if I'm fifteen . . .'

He smiled slightly, as if at some unseen irony. Then he'd said, 'How *do* you feel? Strong enough to go to Africa?' He'd stood up casually.

'Did . . . did you say Africa?' Hannah stammered and sat up again, but this time with the sheet clutched to her throat.

'Well, I think I did,' he said lazily, but with a glint

of devilry in his eye. 'But the way you're holding that sheet up is giving me other ideas.'

'Oh,' Hannah said confusedly and lowered it by about an inch. 'But ... did you ... are you serious?'

'Deadly serious,' he replied gravely and came back to the bed. 'You look so tantalizingly prim and proper, it's an invitation to rip it off.'

'Alex,' she said breathlessly. 'I ...'

'You what, Hannah?' he asked with his eyebrows raised and sat down beside her again. 'Do you think this kind of thing should be reserved for the deep dark hours of the night? Or don't you know how beautiful you are? And that husbands like looking at their wives at just about any time of the day?' He looked at her with mock gravity.

She blushed. 'Maybe it's something I've got to get used to yet,' she said tremulously.

His dark eyes gleamed for a moment. Then he picked up her free hand and kissed her knuckles. 'Maybe,' he said. 'What were we talking about before this?'

'Africa—you asked me if I felt strong enough to go to Africa, but I think you were teasing me.'

He grinned faintly. 'As a matter of fact I was teasing, but not about that. Before you woke I got a phone call advising that I'd got two late cancellations on the South African Airways flight to Johannesburg in three days' time. And with a bit of luck, we'll get all visa formalities completed in time ... From Johannesburg we can make a connection to Nairobi and from there we can, at our leisure, explore places like Mombasa, Malindi, Zanzibar, Dar-es-Salaam—I don't know about the Seychelles and I'm sorry it isn't India ... what is it?'

'Don't,' she begged. 'I can't believe it's true! Do you mean, we came all the way to Perth on the off-chance of getting on the flight?' she asked wonderingly.

'We did. But Perth's not a bad spot anyway,' he teased.

'I know ... And that's why we had those inoculations ...'

'I told you we might go overseas.'

'Yes, but I thought of somewhere close, like Fiji.'

'Would you rather ...'

'No! Oh, how can I say thank you?'

'You don't have to *say* it,' he murmured, looking at her lips.

Hannah lifted her face to his and felt his arms slide round her. 'Was it all right last night, after all?' he said into her hair.

'Yes,' she whispered, suddenly shaken by the memory of it. 'Oh, yes ...'

His mouth sought hers but just as she felt her body softening to his, he lifted his head suddenly and said a little wryly, 'Perhaps we ought to pace ourselves. We have a lot to do over the next few days. What do you think?' He regarded her parted lips and flushed face and she saw the slow smile start at the back of his eyes.

'I think,' she said slowly and very seriously, and paused and put her head to one side consideringly, 'I think—you're probably right!' She twisted out of his arms taking the sheet with her, slipped off the other side of the bed only to trip on her improvised toga and end in a laughing heap on the floor. 'I never could make a dignified exit,' she gasped finally.

Africa.

'A diary,' Hannah said distractedly. 'I need a diary and a camera. I can't believe it. Oh, I know just how Doctor Livingstone and Mr Stanley must have felt!'

'Do you?'

'Well, a little bit,' she confessed with a grin.

'Then we shall definitely have to see you get both,' Alex said amusedly. 'As a matter of fact I never come here myself without a camera, but,' he glanced at her out of the corner of his eye, 'in the heat of the moment I guess it must have been, I forgot it.'

Hannah went pink and he laughed and threw a casual arm around her shoulder. 'When are you going to stop blushing when I say things like that?' he asked. 'I might have to start calling you Rosie soon . . .'

'Don't you dare!' Hannah replied indignantly. 'One day soon,' she added airily, but at the same time, in her heart of hearts, wondered if he wouldn't for ever have the power to make her blush and feel shy. It still seemed unbelievable to her that this tall, sophisticated man who made love to her by night and treated her much like a kid sister by day—except for the odd comments he made out of the blue—could really be her husband.

She thought about it often and it did occur to her that she didn't mind being treated like a kid sister, because she found that easier to handle. It also occurred to her, however, that one reason for this was because something inside her was very, very wary of her losing herself, mind and soul to Alex Cameron . . . Or at least being *seen* to, she reflected once in a moment of clear perception. Because—why? Because you still can't believe he will want to spend the rest of his life with you, Hannah, she acknowledged and felt a chill finger touch her heart, like a presentiment of how it would feel if that day ever came . . .

She always shook herself out of these thoughts determinedly and pledged herself to try and break down the barriers of shyness she still felt.

Africa itself, though, didn't help. A succession of experiences, visual, sensual, so vivid that her imaginings gleaned from all she had read were like pale shadows by comparison made it very hard not to act like an enchanted child let loose in another world. Who could be unaffected by seeing this all for the first time? Zanzibar for example, set like a lovely jewel in the Indian Ocean, with its coral, white beaches and frangipani, its cruel and mysterious past of slave-trading and its exotic mixtures of races. It was impossible not to be moved by it or ever forget it, for more reasons than one . . .

It was also where she reached for the first time, that tantalizing plateau that had beckoned so mysteriously when Alex had made love to her on their wedding night.

He'd hired a boat for the day and they'd found a secluded, deserted beach where they'd swum and eaten a picnic lunch and slept it off through the midday heat. She'd woken to the feel of his hand on her waist and seen the look in his eyes.

Right from the start it had had a quality of momentousness about it. She had sat up slowly and looked around nervously and then looked at him, lifting her hands obediently to take her costume off.

Something about their naked bodies in the sunlight had affected her deeply. She had forgotten any inhibitions or shyness and had lain with her head propped on one elbow so that she could watch his lean brown hands cup her breasts and stroke her nipples and span her waist before sliding down the swell of her hips to her thighs. Then she'd moulded herself to him as if she could not get close enough and moved her hands slowly and lingeringly as he had done, up and down the long, strong lines of his back and

pressed her lips to his shoulder and his throat, tasting
the warm, slightly salty tang of his skin.

The ultimate union of their bodies had fanned the
slow fire at the pit of her stomach, but this time it had
spread so that it was more than a lovely but shadowy
sensation that wasn't quite within her grasp, that
slipped away elusively. This time it had deepened
until the wide world and the white beach beneath her
and the sound of the surf had dropped away, and she
had gasped and hidden her face in his shoulder as he'd
held her close, and her whole body had shuddered
again and again at the beauty and intensity of it.

Then, it could have been hours or it could have
been minutes later, she'd lifted her lashes to see him
staring down at her, and read in those dark eyes that
he'd known this was a first for her, and had heard him
say quietly as he'd smoothed her hair, 'Now you really
are a woman, Hannah.'

A woman, yes, she thought often and found herself
curiously sobered. Several days later she wept, but not
for Alex to see, because she wasn't to be a mother yet.
But although he hadn't seen her tears, he'd known it
all the same and for just an instant she'd got the
feeling he was disappointed too. She managed to
convince herself otherwise without much difficulty,
though, and blamed her flight of fancy on this new
and highly vulnerable state of womanhood for it had
not transformed her overnight into a younger version
of the coolly elegant creature she'd once seen Alex
with in Surfer's . . .

'I didn't know,' she said to herself beneath her
breath one night, when Alex was asleep beside her,
'what it was all about. It's *like* growing up in a day.
It's as if it's set the seal really, on being in love with

him. I know now I could never be any other way but in love with him. But it's more . . . It's as if when I'm happy, I'm happier than I ever thought possible, and when I'm sad I'm sadder . . . It's as if I was only partly alive before. Nobody told me it would be like this. Nobody said anything about the torture of loving and not knowing if you were loved, really loved, the same way, in return.'

She sighed and watched the golden moon that was sailing high over Mombasa.

However, her new sobriety of mind didn't entirely inhibit her capacity for getting herself into trouble, she found, and found herself wondering bleakly if she would ever lose that dubious ability. Because what happened to her made everything else that had ever happened to her pale into insignificance, and it caused Alex to lose his temper with her for the first time since their wedding.

It had all started out like any other day, as did most of the troubled days of her life . . .

If only there was some portent of these things, she thought tearfully, later, but in fact this day had started out even better than most. Why wouldn't it after all, when you were on safari in the heart of East Africa?

'Oh, it's been like a dream come true!' Hannah said aloud to herself, as she looked about their camp site on an escarpment that overlooked the plains of Serengeti. It was a misty morning below, with curls of white cloud lying lazily over the far flung landscape that lay quiet and motionless, tinted wheat-gold and rose-pink in the very early sunlight.

It would be hot down there later, she knew, although at the moment, the air she breathed was cool and sparkling, like champagne. Then she wrinkled her nose appreciatively as the scent of wood smoke drifted down wind, and she knew breakfast was on the way.

This safari had been Alex's idea and right from the
start, Hannah had been entranced. He'd said to her that
there were two ways of going—joining an organised tour
which provided just about every luxury from hot
showers to properly chilled wine with dinner, or, as he
put it—the way it should be done—roughing it.

'Oh, let's rough it,' she'd said laughingly. 'I love the
sound of that! Besides I'm perfectly used to that. I've
roughed it from Cape York to Birdsville with my
father.'

Alex had looked at her shining, enthusiastic face,
not quite smiling and said, 'Plenty of hazards there I
guess.' She'd thought at the time that it had been an
oddly obscure remark to make, but had forgotten it . . .
So they'd hired an acquaintance from a previous trip
of Alex's, a quiet thoughtful man with a surprising
sense of humour and a fund of knowledge about East
Africa and its animals. Sam Carter had supplied all the
equipment—two Land-Rovers and all the camping
gear, and brought along two African assistants. Into
the space of three weeks they'd packed an incredible
amount of sight-seeing and not only of big game, but
also of villages and people.

Hannah's camera had run hot and her delight had
been unbounded. She'd often had to pinch herself as
she photographed Mount Kenya and Kilimanjaro; as
they drove along the floor of the Rift Valley and round
the lip of the N'gorongoro Crater, along the shores of
Lake Victoria—it had been like a dream come true.

Everywhere they'd stopped she'd made friends with
the locals, photographed them and insisted on Alex
photographing her, generally surrounded by children
which earned her the nickname of 'Missy Mama' from
the two Africans accompanying them.

Regretfully, though, today was the last day, she

mused as she helped pack the chop-box after breakfast. Tomorrow it was back to Nairobi and the start of the long trip home. Tonight they would have their last *braai-vleis*—the Afrikaans equivalent of a barbecue, as Sam had explained, and gone on to tell them that he hailed originally from South Africa and spoke Afrikaans fluently.

Could one ever forget the sheer magic of a *braai-vleis*? she thought. The veld, the smell of meat cooking on an open fire that tasted subtly different from when it was cooked on a solid barbecue plate, and the mystery of the whole experience when you were surrounded by an African dusk, with its own subtle scents and strange noises that made your skin prickle when you thought of the animals out there, all around you . . .

The herds of plump zebra with their startling hides and their inseparable comrades-at-arms, wildebeest—less commonly, but more aptly, she often thought, known as gnu; the exquisitely dainty gazelle and a host of other antelope; giraffe, hippo—so many species of animals she couldn't believe it, but she knew she'd never forget her first sighting of a leopard lying lazily in the branch of a tree, or the cheetah they spotted one very early morning. Then there were the big guns as she thought of them, elephant, lion, buffalo and rhino, and the couple of nights Sam had thought it prudent for he and his two helpers to take turns at keeping watch . . . Oh no, one could never forget it.

'Coming, Hannah?' Alex said, breaking into her reverie. 'Or should we leave you here?' He grinned down at her.

'Coming,' she said with a faint sigh and an answering grin, and put her hand into his outstretched one.

It was a flat tyre not long after they'd started driving, which so very nearly precipitated Hannah's demise and a set of over-zealously tightened nuts on the wheel that had seen all four men taking turns at heaving and straining on the wheel brace and using not entirely complimentary language towards not only the stubborn nuts, but also the world in general finally, when the wheel brace broke and they were left with only a spanner . . .

Hannah hid a smile and turned away and decided she'd be just as well employed photographing the view. So she wandered around and soon forgot the irate men as she soaked up the hot stillness of the African bush. It was her last day of it and, in her absorption, she didn't realise she had gone a bit further from the Land-Rover than might have been wise, although she could still hear their voices. And she was lowering her camera when she all but tripped over a lion cub.

'Oh,' she breathed as she stared down at the fluffy ball of fur with its wide mouth and spiky teeth and pink tongue. Then she went cold as the implications of this find hit her . . .

The world was suddenly very still, she realised, no voices, nothing, as she looked up towards a clump of bushes and thorn trees and experienced the absolutely unparalleled sensation of finding herself staring into the yellow eyes of a fully-grown lioness standing about ten feet away.

Oh God, she thought as she swallowed, and was surprised to find she could even do that, oh God, what have I done now . . .

'Hannah . . .' Alex's voice came from behind her, 'walk backwards slowly.'

She broke out into a cold sweat, but did as she was bid and closed her eyes briefly as the lioness's tail extended into a straight bar behind her and she growled, a low, terrifying rumble of sound.

'Keep walking, Hannah,' Sam Carter's voice said from somewhere to her right.

She did, taking each step in an agony of fear and now mesmerised by those yellow eyes. Then she bumped into something—it was Alex. He steadied her and moved her round behind him with purposeful, but contained movements, and he said very quietly, 'Don't panic, just keep walking.'

She took a sobbing breath. 'What about . . .'

'Do it, Hannah!' His words were barely audible, but all the same they flicked her like a whip.

It seemed like an age, but in fact it was only a couple of minutes later that her steps brought her up against the side of the Land-Rover and she was hauled into it by two pairs of black hands.

Then Alex started to retreat and the lioness stood there with her head sunk low now, and her tail whipping slowly from side to side . . .

She was not only focusing on Alex, but also on Sam who was moving back too, but with his rifle still trained on her. Yet, despite the big cat's flickering indecision, Hannah was convinced she was about to launch herself at one or the other of them when another distraction occurred—the cub yawned widely and gambolled across to plonk itself down between its mother's forepaws. Almost simultaneously, Alex and Sam reached the protection of the Land-Rovers. The lioness grunted, bared her teeth in their direction, then dropped her head and lifted the cub by the scruff of the neck, turned and disappeared into the thicket.

Hannah wiped the sweat off her face and started to shake uncontrollably as Alex climbed into the back of the Land-Rover.

'You fool,' he said, his dark eyes blazing with anger. 'You stupid, thoughtless, little fool. Will you ever learn any sense?' He reached across and hauled her to her knees unceremoniously. 'You've been out here for three weeks yet you still haven't grasped the simplest, most basic law—not to wander off on your own. I can't let you out of my sight for a minute. What you need is a bloody good hiding, Hannah, because you see, not only did you place your own life in danger but also Sam's, mine and the lioness's if Sam had had to shoot her, and then her cub's. All because you, Hannah Hawthorn, never stop to *think*!'

Hannah stared up at him, her face stricken and with tears pouring down her cheeks. 'I'm sorry,' she said desperately.

'*Sorry*.' He looked at her contemptuously and shook her violently. 'Isn't it time you grew up and stopped having to apologise to people?' And he shook her again until she felt her teeth rattle.

'Please,' she whispered, 'I feel sick . . .'

And sick she was, with her head shoved over the side of the Land-Rover ignominiously, but when it was over, Alex seemed to have cast off the worst of his rage because he wet a towel from the water bottle and cleaned her up, himself, as if she was a child, although his eyes were still cold and she knew she wasn't forgiven.

All of which cast an effective damper on the day, to say the least, although no one mentioned the incident to her and for the most part, they all tried to act as if it had never happened.

Hannah retired early to bed that night, heartsick and incredibly weary, only to find herself unable to sleep. She lay for a long time on the inflatable mattress she and Alex shared, watching the firelight flicker on the walls of the tent.

Perhaps because she'd looked so tired, Alex and
Sam who were still sitting outside over the fire, didn't
bother to lower their voices after a while.

'Man,' she heard Sam say, 'lions are funny,
unpredictable creatures. I could write a book about
them. In fact, after the little incident with Hannah
today, I reckon I will!'

'Perhaps that's what I should do, write a book,'
Alex said drily. 'Hannah seems to attract trouble.'

Hannah winced at the shaft of pain that pierced her
heart.

'Ag now, as they say back home,' Sam replied after
a moment, 'sure, I for one thought she was a goner
until I got my hands on the gun, but she didn't mean
any harm.'

'She never does.'

'You were very hard on her,' Sam continued
thoughtfully. 'Tell you what I think—know I
shouldn't butt in, but I feel as I've got a vested
interest after nearly losing her like that—I think she's
a beaut person, as they say over your way, and I really
mean that,' he said with quiet sincerity. 'But I think
she needs kids. Hey, you only have to look at the way
she attracts them wherever she goes and not only the
two-legged variety,' he added with a chuckle. 'She's a
born mother, our Missy Mama, I reckon.'

It was some time before Alex spoke and when he
did, it sounded as if he was choosing his words
carefully. 'She's very young. I sometimes wonder if it
would . . . be fairer to her to wait.'

'She's not that young,' Sam said surprisingly. 'She
might be a whole lot more grown up inside than you
give her credit for. Still, it *is* none of my business.
Wonder how many cubs Lady Leo had snookered
away in that patch of bush . . .'

Hannah listened for a while longer, concentrating carefully because she didn't want to have to think about what Alex had said, and drifted off to sleep without knowing it.

She woke very early the next morning and found Alex already awake beside her and watching her in the grey light of an overcast dawn.

For a time he said nothing, just stared down into her wary eyes. Then a shadow of a smile touched his lips and he said, 'Shall we be friends today, Missy Mama?' He reached out to cup her cheek in his hand.

She swallowed the lump in her throat. 'Yes . . . oh, yes please.'

CHAPTER SIX

'Oh well,' Marge Riley said, as she glanced around the littered dining room of the big house, 'I guess we'll have to forgive you two for *sneaking* off and getting married. All these beautiful presents you brought back ... What do you say, folks?' she asked at large.

All of the Rileys and nearly all of the Watsons and Billy Johnson expressed agreement in one form or another. Even Mrs Hunter smiled primly, so it was left to Master Richard Watson to disagree.

'I never been to a wedding,' he said aggrievedly.

'I'm sorry, Richard,' Alex said gravely. 'Do you like your present though?'

'Yep. Do you like yours?'

'Yep ...'

'Richard, you're supposed to say thank you, not—yep!' his mother admonished. 'We all should ...'

'For that matter, Hannah and I would like to thank you all for this lovely gift.' Alex glanced at the engraved set of silver cutlery that held pride of place on the table. 'It's magnificent, and this surprise party to welcome us home has been as good as a wedding, don't you agree, Hannah?'

'Certainly,' she said gravely.

Richard thought for a moment before saying, 'Does that mean you're going to let him kiss you, Hannah?'

'Richard!' several voices chorused but Alex ignored them and turned Hannah to face him and kissed her on the lips.

'There,' he said. 'Satisfied?'

From the applause it appeared everybody was, although Billy Johnson, who had carried off the embarrassment he quite naturally felt rather well, and had in fact recovered better than he'd thought he would from the sheer shock of hearing that Hannah had married Alex, clenched his hands suddenly and looked away. One thing about it, though, he found himself thinking, it's got her out of the hands of that bastard Matt Bartholomew. I notice he's not hanging round no more!

Hannah noticed this fact too and was very relieved but it was only when she was going through the mail one morning that she discovered the reason for this—Tiara Tahiti and the other horses Matt Bartholomew and Alex had owned in partnership, had now passed into Alex's sole ownership. She bit her lip as she realised just how much this must have cost Alex and how it could have meant the loss of Tiara to the stable if Matt Bartholomew had refused to give up his share in the filly. She wasn't to know that her red-headed tormentor, when faced with a coldly angry Alex Cameron whom he hardly recognised, had decided in the interests of staying alive, to part with his share quite equitably . . .

In time, Hannah's concern over this diminished, as did her other secret causes for concern. Such as her nervous certainty that Marge Riley must divine the true nature of this marriage—and that Mrs Hunter might look back and wonder as well. Whatever Marge's thoughts were on the subject, she never gave any intimation of them and continued to treat Hannah as she always had, as a friend and sometimes as a daughter. So Hannah began to relax and even more so when Mrs Hunter got over her slight stiffness of manner, which Hannah realised gradually was not because of any moral distaste she felt, but had been simply designed to show Hannah that she didn't altogether appreciate having an eighteen year old girl dictating to her.

So, all in all, life slipped into a groove that wasn't outwardly very different from what it had been before the day a little girl had fallen off her bike and unwittingly set some surprising wheels in motion.

Yet there were unseen differences, and not only the obvious ones, as Hannah grew more and more into Alex's life. She found that as each day went past, it got harder to preserve any part of herself untouched by him as a protection against the day when he might tire of her and turn away from her. In a sense, this was a good thing, she realised. Because it was like a laying down of arms for her, something she couldn't help, but curiously it brought her a sense of peace and serenity and that in turn helped her to feel more on an equal footing with her tall, assured husband. She began to acquire an added beauty too, like a bloom which everyone saw.

Then two things happened, one of which wasn't so surprising, but the other like the proverbial bolt from the blue. It hit one morning over breakfast when she spoke to Alex twice and received such non-committal replies, she couldn't help but be taken aback.

Then he got up and walked out with his breakfast half eaten, leaving Hannah casting her mind's eye anxiously over her activities of the past few days, but coming to the conclusion that she'd been a model of virtue, for her . . .

Then her old concern about the money he'd spent buying Tiara Tahiti out, coming on top of what must have been a vastly expensive honeymoon, came back to plague her. She had no doubt that Alex was wealthy, but after a lifetime of frugality, she couldn't help worrying about it. She picked up the morning paper he'd left beside his plate to see if there was any gloomy financial news in it—yearling prices and real estate being rather like a barometer of the economy.

The newspaper was open at the social page, she found, and was about to turn it over when a name leapt out of the print at her. Alison Wandsworth née Fairleigh . . .

'Alison—Fairleigh?' she said out aloud with a tiny frown of concentration etched on her forehead. 'Alison . . . oh!' Her eyes widened as they scanned the caption beneath the photo of a lovely, slim, fair woman. 'Alison Wandsworth née Fairleigh,' she read, 'has come out of seclusion following the death of her husband from a rare disease. Charles Wandsworth was struck down in his prime three months ago, but right until the end, at his insistence, very few people knew of the tragedy that had befallen this handsome couple. Mrs Wandsworth was captured above, holidaying on the Gold Coast, and was persuaded to admit that she is taking up the threads of her life again because it was what her husband would have wanted for her. She also said she was endowing a foundation to promote research into the disease which had claimed Charles Wandsworth's life and about which very little is known.'

Hannah let the paper fall and stared unseeingly at the wall opposite.

'What I came up for,' Marge said comfortably a couple of hours later, 'was to ask if I could borrow your paper. Ours, mysteriously, met a soggy end this morning.' She sipped her tea.

'What kind of a soggy end?' Hannah asked after a moment and set her own cup down carefully.

Marge said wryly, 'It was found floating face down in the bath. By whose hand this foul deed was done—is the mystery bit. Everyone claims innocence and I just didn't have the energy to pursue the enquiry.'

'I . . . I think it's here somewhere,' Hannah said vaguely. 'What did you want it for?'

'Well, the Nerang rodeo is on next weekend. It's quite an event. Have you been to one?'

'No—I mean, not here, although I've been to some out west. Well!' she made a conscious effort to inject some enthusiasm into her voice. 'I bet the kids are excited . . . but I don't think there was anything in the paper about it. Not that I saw,' she added and winced inwardly.

Marge shrugged and stayed on to chat, seemingly unaware that anything was wrong although she did say when she left, 'You all right?'

'Fine!'

'You look a bit peaky. There's some kind of a bug going round, I had to keep Sally home from school today . . .'

'Oh? Nothing serious I hope?'

'Don't think so. See you later, love.'

While Hannah breathed a sigh of relief several times that day, she was not to know that Marge bethought herself of the paper she hadn't read again, and went across to Jean Watson's to borrow hers. Which was how, when Mick Riley came home for his lunch, it was to find his wife staring down at the social page with a suddenly dawning look of comprehension in her eyes, which turned into a look of rather horrified guilt as she glanced up at him.

'What's up now?' Mick asked resignedly.

'I ... I think I might have put my foot in my mouth,' Marge said unhappily. 'But at the time I just had no idea!'

'No idea of what?'

'Of Hannah and—Alex,' Marge said helplessly.

'Is something wrong, Hannah?'

Hannah came out of her preoccupation with a start at Alex's words. It was several days after her stunned discovery of a certain revelation in the morning paper of that day.

They were preparing for bed. At least, Hannah still was. Alex was already there, lying with his hands joined behind his head, watching her brush her hair.

The night was warm and windy and the curtains were billowing inwards, just as they'd done on a morning about three months ago, and there was the same smell of orange blossom in the room. Not that it was the same room, because she and Alex shared the master bedroom, but it was on the same side of the house, above the grove of orange and lemon trees.

'No, nothing,' she said, and her eyes sought his, but via the dressing table mirror—to see that his expression gave nothing away in the lamplight. 'Why do you ask?' she said after a moment and forced herself to go on brushing her hair.

'I don't know,' he answered after a moment. 'Perhaps—while you look quite bewitchingly lovely in that nightgown—just, not altogether the Hannah I know.'

Hannah lowered her brush and glanced down at the misty blue-grey nightgown she wore and sometimes thought was too beautiful to wear, with its simply cut vee-necked bodice and layer upon layer of exquisite lace. It was part of the trousseau they'd bought the

day they'd flown to Africa and Alex had chosen it
because of the colour, which, he'd said, matched her
eyes.

'What do you mean?' she asked. 'That it's too . . .
sophisticated for me?'

He smiled faintly. 'Not at all. It's perfect for you
actually. Lovely, fresh and quite unrevealing in a
way—almost prim. That's not what I meant, though. I
thought you seemed to have been very serious lately.
Serious and grown-up. Want to tell me about it?'

'I . . .' She bit her lip. Then she said quietly,
'Perhaps I am growing up at last. I'm nearly nineteen
now.'

He didn't say anything for a while, and she couldn't
quite bring herself to meet his eyes in the mirror. She
put the brush down carefully and stood up and some
impulse made her reach out suddenly and almost
clumsily to switch off the lamp so that the room was in
darkness, save for the starlight coming through the
open curtains.

For some moments she stood uncertainly in the
middle of the room, until she heard him move and say,
'Then why don't you come to bed and show me how
grown-up you've become? Otherwise I'll be tempted
to prefer how you were before the full weight of nearly
twenty summers fell upon you and you got all grave
and serious.'

Hannah felt her heart beat uncomfortably. She
pressed her hands together. 'I thought you did want
me to grow up,' was all she could think of to say.
'You've told me that often enough . . .'

'Come here, Hannah,' he commanded quietly.

She moved towards the bed and sat down.

'I mean really here,' he murmured and reached up
to pull her down beside him, 'in my arms where I can

feel you and maybe find out what's going on behind that . . . give-nothing-away expression I've seen in your eyes lately.'

He pushed his fingers through her hair and tilted her head back so that he could kiss her throat and her shoulders and slide his mouth down towards the hollow between her breasts.

She closed her eyes and forced herself to try to think. But the truth of the matter was, she didn't know what to think. He himself had been perfectly normal since that morning. As if nothing earth-shattering had happened to his world although at the time she'd got the devastating impression that reading about Alison Fairleigh had affected him deeply. Then, she mused, what *could* he do about it? Cast me out forthwith? Surely I know him too well to know he wouldn't do that. So, perhaps he's just making the best of a horribly ironical situation, not realising that I know that the one great love of his life is free now, when he is not . . .

'Hannah?'

Her eyes flew open. 'Yes?' she whispered.

'Now I'm really worried,' he said wryly and reached out to flick on the bedside lamp so that she could see the quizzical glint in his eyes. 'I've just spoken to you twice and you haven't even heard me. Do I have a competitor? Is that it?'

'A . . .?' Her eyes widened. 'Oh! No!'

'Then what, my lovely, passionate child, is exercising your thoughts to this extent? You told me once you had a one track mind. I see now that you were right. Or,' his eyes narrowed suddenly and she tensed, 'are you trying to tell me you don't like what I'm doing to you? Because I'd find that hard to believe,' he added very quietly and let his dark gaze roam from her eyes to her slightly parted lips and down to the satiny skin of her breasts gleaming like ivory in the lamplight above the froth of lace that lay taut over her nipples.

A tangle of thoughts filled Hannah's mind. Will I always be a child to him? How could I bear to lose him, even if he does think of me as a child and doesn't know that no child could possibly feel the way I do . . .

'Hannah . . .'

Alex's voice jolted her out of her chaotic reverie and for the first time since this impossible conversation had started, there was a note of sternness in it so that she flushed and felt her nerves tighten as she saw a corresponding severity in the set of his mouth, as if he wasn't going to let her go on compromising with the truth.

She spoke breathlessly, words straight from her heart and it was only later that she realised how they could be misconstrued. 'If,' she licked her lips, 'say one day we got tired of each other, what would we do? Would you . . . if it happened to you, would you tell me?'

His forehead contracted in a frown as he stared down at her. Then his lips tightened, his fingers bit into her shoulders momentarily and he said harshly, 'What's that supposed to mean?'

'N-nothing really,' she stammered. 'I just wanted to know.'

'Hannah,' he said grimly, 'only a fool asks that kind of a question with absolutely no motivation. Although you often do foolish things, you don't normally talk like a fool. So I'd like to know what the hell's going on. No,' he warned quietly, but with undisguised menace as she tried to turn her head away, 'don't do that. I want to know what all this is about and I will, if I have to shake it out of you.'

She lay quite still and the colour drained from her face leaving her eyes huge and dark, and a bitter little sob rose up in her throat. 'I hate you sometimes, Alex,' she said unsteadily. 'You always *treat* me as if I was a child!'

'Do I?' he countered coolly. 'Forgive me then but I must admit I'm confused because I thought I was treating you very much like a woman—perhaps a young and inexperienced one, but then that's what you are and I thought you'd prefer it that way. We can always change it though, if you don't. But I'd still like to know what's made you see things differently.'

'It's ... I ... you don't understand ...' She tailed off and flinched at the look of savage impatience that crossed his face.

'*Hannah*, are you trying to tell me in a roundabout kind of way that you're tired of me?'

'No,' she whispered frantically. 'It's not that ... well ... no ...' She stumbled, and couldn't go on.

'Then why have you changed?' he asked mercilessly, his eyes cold and piercing. 'It hasn't been only tonight. I noticed it days ago. *Have* you met someone else?'

'*No* ...'

'Then you've come to the conclusion that you'd be better off without me. Which only goes to show,' he said through his teeth, 'my dear child who doesn't like to be called that, just how foolish you can be.'

For a second Hannah forgot her miserable confusion in the hot tide of rage that rose up within her. And it found an unexpected outlet that took her almost by surprise. She wrenched herself free and struck him across the face and raised her hand to do it again with a wild little sob of fury, but he caught her wrist in a brutal grip and ruthlessly dragged it down.

She struggled briefly and then subsided panting, and swallowed suddenly at what she saw in his eyes ...

'Well, well, so you too have a violent temper, Hannah,' he said speaking quietly and dispassionately. 'Another besetting sin to add to your list. I'm sure if we were to quote your father on the subject, he would have said that sometimes you have to pay for your sins. Perhaps it won't be ... inappropriate, in view of what you won't tell me beyond this business of being treated like a child and not a woman. Maybe this is what you want?'

And with movements as deliberate and unhurried as his words, he released her wrists and brought his hands up and tore her nightgown from the neckline to the hem and laid it open on either side of her. Then he studied the whole pale length of her leisurely and with a gleam of sardonic amusement in his eyes as they came back to rest on her stunned face.

'I've been very gentle with you, Hannah,' he murmured, 'in deference to your youth and innocence, but perhaps the time has come to up the tempo. Maybe that's what you need to keep you out of mischief.'

'Alex,' she whispered shakily, but he only glanced at her agonised eyes briefly then lowered his mouth to hers. What followed was quite different from any of the ways he'd made love to her before. Mainly because there was a quality of detachment about him that made him seem like a stranger and worse, because she sensed he was going to make her respond to him whether she wanted to or not ...

All the same, she tried not to. She tensed every muscle in her body stubbornly, but he broke through her defences one by one with his hands and his lips until she realised despairingly that passive rigidity was not the answer, but a trap for her own body in fact. She felt herself relaxing and was filled with a curious sense of inadequacy when he raised his head briefly and she saw the mocking look in his eyes. Not only that, but also a bitter sense of hurt in her heart that he should want it this way . . .

None of this altered the fact that where he led, her body followed and she moved within the circle of his arms to the rhythm of desire and arched herself against him and gasped with pleasure when he kissed her breasts and led her towards that astonishingly lovely sensation she'd come into possession of for the first time on a white beach off Africa. This time though it was only to draw her back each time as she trembled on the brink of it and start another devastating assault on her senses, so skilfully and relentlessly. This subtle torture went on until she whispered his name over and over again, pleading, gasping, because she couldn't stand the exquisite torment of it any more, she thought.

It took a long time to come back from those unbelievable heights they finally reached together, but at last their bodies were still and he rolled away from her.

She didn't move, just lay there with her eyes wide and tearless, her limbs lax like a rag doll's and her breath catching in her throat. She didn't want to move, didn't think she could, in fact, and she didn't want to think. But finally a slight sound pierced the numb blackness of her mind and she turned her head very slowly to find Alex propped up on one elbow and staring down at her sombrely.

A slow tide of colour crept into her cheeks as she thought of the shameless, almost wanton way she'd reacted even while she'd known he was taking her in a kind of anger. Something Matt Bartholomew had once said to her suddenly slid into her dazed mind—about an orang-utan playing a violin—but this had been the opposite, she thought bleakly. She had been a novice in the hands of a master and he had played her mercilessly, deliberately, until she'd been mindless and powerless to resist and more, totally dominated in a way she'd not thought possible, by what he'd done to her—by him.

She closed her eyes and could never remember feeling more defenceless or vulnerable. Or for that matter, more exhausted and confused.

'Hannah?'

She turned her head away and felt the tears slide down her cheeks.

'Don't cry,' he said brusquely. 'Isn't that what you wanted?'

She didn't answer, just moved her head in a gesture that could have been despair, and licked the salty tears from her lips and tensed nervously as he slid his arms around her body and gathered her close.

'Oh God,' he said very quietly, 'I'm *sorry*. I knew you weren't ready for that. One day you'll understand ... Don't cry,' he said again, but this time very gently and he smudged the tears from her eyelashes.

She couldn't help herself, though, and she wept into his shoulder. He let her cry and stroked her hair. Then, when the sobbing had subsided at last, he began to talk to her, soothingly ...

'Remember Nairobi airport, Hannah? And how astonished you were to find it was in the middle of a game reserve. Remember all the *braais* we had in the bush and the way the moonlight shone on Kilimanjaro that night? And that black baby you wanted to kidnap and the Masai tribesman who looked as if he'd like to kidnap you? Do you remember ...'

And he evoked a host of recollections, sometimes teasingly and occasionally with an odd note in his voice she couldn't identify. Until she found herself relaxing involuntarily and finally, even smiling shakily. Then she fell asleep in his arms and didn't know that he went on talking for a little while and stroking her hair until he was sure she wouldn't waken. For a long time he stared down at the fragile beauty of her body that bore the unmistakable marks of his possession of it, and then he closed his eyes briefly before reaching out to switch off the lamp.

She slept late the next morning—so late that Alex was up and gone when Mrs Hunter finally woke her.

'Well, Hannah,' she said. 'Lazy days make for lazy ways and you certainly are making this a lazy day. Still, Alex said to leave you a while, but the most interesting thing has happened!'

'Oh?' Hannah reached for the sheet only to find herself tucked up most modestly. She stared at the breakfast tray Mrs Hunter had put down on the bed. 'You shouldn't have bothered . . . what do you mean? What's happened?'

'Well I got a phone call from a reporter just after Alex had left,' Mrs Hunter said mysteriously. 'Shall I pour the tea or will you wait until you've eaten your egg?'

'I . . . um . . . yes thanks. I don't feel very hungry,' Hannah said confusedly. 'What did the reporter want?'

'He wanted to know if there was any truth in the rumour that the Wandsworth property was to be auctioned lock stock and barrel and whether Alex was going to handle it?' Mrs Hunter said triumphantly, She went on, 'Seems he got it from—what did he say—impeccable sources, that the widow has put it on the market, at least in Alex's hands. What do you think of that? I can tell you it will cause a bit of a stir! Charles Wandsworth's ancestors opened up that area, did you know? But not only that, according to this reporter! Apparently there's a lot of bitterness in the family about it being sold. Fancy that,' she said with the peculiarly avid look of a person who loved nothing so much as a good gossip.

Hannah tried to think of something to say, but failed and sipped her tea instead with a strange, sinking feeling in her heart.

'Of course it's quite natural Alex should handle it,' Mrs Hunter went on undeterred. 'He knows her—the widow I mean. She was a Fairleigh and the prettiest thing you ever laid eyes on. And according to . . .' Mrs Hunter stopped abruptly and went faintly pink but was saved from further embarrassment by the far away peal of the telephone. 'Drat!' she said and stood up hastily. 'If it's reporters again what shall I say? Or,' she hesitated, 'don't you know anything about it either?'

Hannah would have given anything to be able to deny this for more reasons than one, and one of lesser ones being that she and Mrs Hunter weren't precisely kindred spirits, although they got along well enough. She said steadily, 'No, I don't. Did Alex say where he was going?' Mrs Hunter shook her head. 'Then you'd better refer them to the office in town, Mrs Hunter. I'll be down just now to give you a hand.'

It was some time before Hannah got downstairs, in fact. She set her tea down as Mrs Hunter left the room and lay back to stare up at the ceiling, unseeingly.

'Now this,' she whispered. 'On top of last night. What does it mean? He's obviously seen her, spoken to her . . . Could it be that it wasn't only me he got angry about last night? Was there a sense of frustration in it too?'

She lay there for some time, trying to think. Then she heard the phone ringing again and, with an effort, got up and took a shower.

It was the sight of her naked body in the long bathroom mirror afterwards, that brought some cohesion to her thoughts although not particularly in connection Alison Farleigh Wandsworth, nor very happily. As she stared at her reflection and shivered slightly as she thought of Alex's hands moving on her as they'd done last night, and as she touched her fingers to a faint pattern of bruises on her upper arm that would correspond exactly to the imprint of his lean, strong fingers, and the other small signs that he had not been gentle with her last night, a curious feeling invaded her. Or a mixture of feelings, she thought with a sigh. A humiliatingly feminine one, because she'd responded as she had, but then in an odd way, proudly so too. Why? she wondered. Shouldn't I hate him for deliberately setting out to show me how little I knew, how—childish and unversed I must seem to him and maybe always will . . .

'But the truth is I don't,' she said out aloud to her reflection. 'I feel . . . confused, as always, but not out of love with him, not that. Still caught and held fast by him even when I might not want to be. Is this,' her grey eyes were shadowed and painfully questioning in the mirror, 'is this what it really means to be a woman . . .?'

When Alex got home that night, late, she was already in bed. He came straight up to the bedroom and sat down beside her and took her into his arms. She trembled, thought of resisting, but in the end laid her head on his shoulder.

'I'm sorry I'm late,' he said after a while. 'Are you all right?'

She nodded wordlessly.

He tilted her chin up and studied her face. 'You don't . . . look all right,' he said with a crooked little smile. 'You look,' he sobered, 'worried. About last night, Hannah, I'd give anything to be able to undo that, but I too, as you know, have a temper.' He touched her face with his fingers. 'I couldn't work out what you were trying to get at. Want to tell me now?'

'I think,' she whispered, then took a breath and found she couldn't tell him any more than she could last night, 'I think, I still sometimes can't believe that this, us—you and I—is real . . .' Which *was* the truth in a way.

'Then I'll have to show you,' he said very quietly. 'Before that, though, I'll have to tell you that I love you, Hannah, and you mustn't ever doubt it . . .'

'You don't have to say that.'

'Why not? It's true.'

She hid her face in his shoulder and thought, yes it's true in a way, I know that, but is it the same kind of love you . . . you had with her?

'Hannah?'

She lifted her head at last and knew what she had to do—if she couldn't tell him her real fears, what else was there to do? 'I love you too,' she said gruffly, and smiled shakily.

'Then, would you mind if I . . . tried to make up for last night?'

'No . . .'

Which he did, but so gently, she cried again but this

time with the warm harmony of it, and felt deep in her heart that there was something very special about this lovemaking. Which, as it turned out, there was . . .

The next day, quite in the normal course of events, Alex told her about the sale of the Wandsworth property, and how, because of the historic aspect of it not to mention the amount of money it represented, he'd decided to launch a nation-wide advertising campaign of the auction. He also told her a bit about the opposition Alison Wandsworth was encountering from the family over the sale.

'Does . . .' Hannah said hesitatingly, 'does she not have any children? Because if she does, might they not think of it as part of their heritage?'

'No. In fact, there's no young blood in the family at present, but a lot of fairly elderly aunts and uncles and cousins who love the prestige of it, but would probably tremble at the thought of actually having to run it—especially with a drought looming. She's the major share-holder, though, and has the final say. Unfortunately, the drought isn't going to make it very easy to sell. So I'm going to have to spend a lot of time on it . . .'

And it was, in fact, the amount of time he spent on the sale of the Wandsworth property, which enabled Hannah, several weeks later, to discover that she was pregnant and be the sole possessor of the knowledge of it. For a time anyway.

CHAPTER SEVEN

IT was Marge who was the first to know. She came up to spend the evening with Hannah and found her getting rid of her evening meal in a rather painful manner. Alex was away in Sydney.

'I must have eaten something that disagreed with me,' Hannah said, wiping the sweat off her forehead. 'But it happened last night too . . .'

Marge's eyes narrowed thoughtfully, then she said carefully, 'Sometimes it takes one this way.'

'What does?'

'A baby . . .'

Hannah looked up and saw there was no point in dissembling. 'Do you mean I'm having morning sickness at night?'

'A lot of women do.'

'Then,' Hannah said weakly, 'why is it called morning sickness? And how did you know?'

'I didn't *know*. I suspected though,' Marge said gently. 'There's something about your first pregnancy that puts you into a sort of daze, as if you don't know whether you're on your head or your heels. Especially . . .'

'Especially me? I suppose that follows,' Hannah said, with a curious sense of resignation.

'Oh, nonsense!' Marge replied forcefully. 'Especially when you're only eighteen was what I was going to say.'

Hannah smiled slightly. Then she said quietly, 'I'm nearly nineteen now. Which means that by the time this baby is born I'll be nearly twenty. That's not so young to have a baby, is it?'

Marge stared at her. 'Does Alex know?'

'No . . .'

Marge frowned. 'Is something wrong? I thought you'd be thrilled . . . Hannah . . .'

Hannah turned away from what she saw in Marge's eyes, something that had been there for weeks now. And she knew what it was that was making Marge so concerned—the subject of Alison Fairleigh. She started to change the subject, but Marge was not be gainsaid this time . . .

'Hannah,' she said, 'I can't go on any longer ignoring this. Especially when I can see that you're so . . . confused and unhappy now . . .'

'I'm not.'

'Then why haven't you told Alex about the baby?'

'I . . .'

'Hannah, believe me, I'd give my right arm to be able to go back and unsay all that I did to you about Alex and Alison Fairleigh,' Marge said unsteadily. 'But I didn't know. Not that it's any excuse.'

Hannah was silent. Then she said, 'How could you have known? I didn't know myself. It was the last thing I expected, that Alex would . . . marry me.'

'Then . . .' Marge tried to frame the question, but found she couldn't. 'I don't want to pry,' she said painfully.

'Why did I marry him? Because I fell in love with him. I did exactly what you both tried to warn me about and what I was so certain couldn't happen to me. Then, something happened which—convinced Alex I couldn't take care of myself and, he decided to marry me, I think mostly out of a sense of obligation to my father. What . . . none of us could have known, the irony of it,' she said huskily, 'was that almost to the day he married me, Alison Fairleigh . . . became free.'

'Hannah . . .' Marge stopped and started again. 'You seem very sure he doesn't love you, but anyone with eyes in their head could see that he's terribly fond of you!'

'Oh he loves me in . . . in that kind of way . . .'

'How many kind of ways are there?'

'I think there are a lot of different ways,' Hannah said very quietly. 'I think, when you've lost your heart to someone, but there's no hope, you—you make do with someone else, perhaps. I . . . can't help knowing, in a special sort of way,' she coloured, but went on resolutely, 'that Alex and I aren't, well, equals, as true lovers should be, I think. I know he'd never . . . abandon me because he feels so responsible for me in so many ways. And now with this baby . . .' She tailed off, and shrugged.

Marge sighed, then she said, surprisingly sternly, 'Now let's just be realistic about this. Oh God! I will never indulge in idle gossip again,' she said bitterly. 'But don't you see, Hannah, you're *assuming* an awful lot. For starters you're assuming that Alex still feels the same way he did fifteen years ago—that's a hell of a long time—and that she still feels the same way. Or do you have some proof of it?' Marge demanded.

'Not—no,' Hannah said. 'But where am I going to find tangible proof of it? That's the last thing Alex would do to me . . .'

'But don't you see that's like convicting someone without evidence. That's not fair! So until *some* proof hits you on the head, what you've got to do is go back to how you were before you picked up the morning paper one day and saw her picture—oh yes, I did finally get hold of that paper,' Marge said to Hannah's startled look. 'You did a good job of fooling me at the time, not that it was necessary with the sale of the place coming up,' she added with an angry sort of compassion, the anger directed at herself. 'You've got to go back to how you were then . . .'

'Do you think I don't want to?' Hannah said with sudden passion. 'Do you think I'm not trying to? Do you think when I first knew about this baby, I wasn't so happy because . . . because it has to be a bond, a real bond between us. Do you think . . . do you have any idea of the awful thoughts I have sometimes?' she asked, her voice sinking suddenly. 'That I'm glad she's lost her chance because . . . because she had a much better chance than I ever had, and she just doesn't deserve Alex. But I *hate* myself for thinking like that . . .'

'Honey, you don't *know* they're . . .'

'Marge,' Hannah said wearily, 'you mustn't blame yourself for this. You see, you weren't the only one who told me he lost his heart to her.'

Marge's eyes widened. 'Who?'

'It doesn't matter . . .'

'Hannah.' Marge slumped tiredly too. 'You're *right* about one thing, though,' she said, taking heart. 'This baby will be a bond.'

Hannah stared at her hands. 'He . . . Alex thinks I'm too young to have children, and I do have proof about that. I heard him say it . . .'

The curious thing is, though, Hannah thought a day or two after her conversation with Marge, I might not be able to fool Marge, but I seem to be fooling Alex lately. Or is it just that he's so busy recently, he hasn't had time to see that things didn't really come

right that night, the night I got my baby ... I don't
know how I can be sure of that but I seem to be ...

Or perhaps he thinks he's done what he can to ...
reassure me, and the rest is up to me now? Which is
true. It is up to me ...

Accordingly, she made a determined effort to lift
herself above the turmoil of her soul, with some
success, although she still hadn't told Alex that she
was pregnant.
'I'll do it tonight, she told herself on a sunny
Saturday. Alex was in Sydney again, this time at a
dispersal sale, but he was due home that afternoon.

With the decision finally made, she found herself
feeling more relaxed than she had for some time and
when Sally Riley came up, they baked a couple of
cakes and a ton of biscuits, which always went down
well with the Riley and Watson children who all
congregated on the front lawn and begged Hannah to
get out her guitar and mouth-organ.

Which she did and she organised cold drinks and it
was only after she'd been playing for a while that she
put her guitar down suddenly and said, 'Where's
Richard? Never known him not to be able to scent out
a chocolate cake!'

Richard's elder brother Greg pulled a face. 'He's got
a mate from school over. They're playing cops and
robbers in the feed shed. With a bit of luck they'll stay
there all afternoon. I'm supposed to be keeping an eye
on 'em,' he added lugubriously and received some
sympathetic mutters in return.

'Where are Mum and Dad?' Hannah asked.

'Gone to the races with Billy and Mick. We've got
four starters today.' Greg rolled on to his back on the
soft grass. 'I wish they'd taken Richard too. That child
needs a transmitter sewn into him so that you could

keep track of him,' he said with the wisdom of all his twelve years.

Hannah grinned. 'I know what you mean. And perhaps you ought to go and check on them. They could get into lovely trouble in the feed shed if they were so minded. Remember what happened last week?'

Everyone groaned feelingly because last week Master Richard Watson had distinguished himself by pouring a mixture of sand and water into the petrol tanks of several of the property vehicles, thereby rendering them useless. He had said in his defence that he'd seen it done on 'telly' and had wondered if it really worked.

'Worked what?' his furious father had yelled at him.

'Made them not go! See, this bloke had these crooks chasing after him and he wanted to stop their car from working . . . it does work,' he had added ingenuously, and had had to be removed from his father's orbit for some time.

Yes, Hannah thought, as she cleared up the remains of the impromptu picnic, a transmitter in that small person might help. Then, a few minutes later, she glanced out of the kitchen window and noted a search party in operation, led by Greg.

She sighed, having not infrequently been involved in a search for Richard herself—a tedious, time-consuming business, particularly if he didn't want to be found.

Yet for some reason as she stood and watched, she felt a prickle of fear run down her spine, and she found herself thinking of the creek. She couldn't say why, except perhaps for the fact that Richard never willingly missed out on a music session either, which he would have been able to hear from most parts of the property . . . but not the creek, perhaps.

'No,' she said out aloud. 'Surely not?' For the creek was strictly out of bounds for the younger children unless accompanied by an adult.

The thought persisted uncomfortably. With a friend to goad him on, one who didn't realise this was an inflexible rule . . . well, maybe, she mused. Anyway, it won't do any harm to check. And if they are there, I'll probably find them making mud pies or doing something equally harmless.

Not fifteen minutes later, however, this was proved to be a vain hope. She had some intimation of it as she walked through the hot, still bush to the closest bank. Then she heard a faint cry. She broke into a run and felt a cold sweat break out on her forehead as she reached the bank and saw, with some surprise, how swiftly the creek was flowing, and realised there must have been rain upstream.

'Richard!' she called, and the faint cry came again to her right. She swung in that direction and stumbled through the undergrowth towards it.

The scene that met her eyes as she came round a bend, all but took her breath away. Richard was kneeling on a crudely constructed raft in mid-stream, desperately trying to reach out for a branch that the other child, who was standing in the shallows, was holding out to him. The branch wasn't quite long enough, though, and as she stood still for one petrified instant, Richard leant as far forward as he could, the raft tilted up beneath him and he fell into the water with it on top of him.

Hannah was galvanised into action. 'You go and get help!' she called to the other child and stopping long enough only to take her shoes off, she waded into the water and then began to dive beneath the raft.

The water was murky and full of debris washed

down from upstream and the raft banged into her once, all but taking her breath away. Then she saw a fair head surface some way from her—it was Richard with his mouth wide open, taking great gulps of air but being swept away on the current . . .

She swam more desperately than she ever had in her life, using every ounce of strength she possessed. And reached him, but then she had to get them both back to the bank, against the current.

She never knew how she made it but perhaps it was the feel of Richard's limp body in her arms that spurred her on.

Then, out of the blue, just as her feet scraped the bottom, a strong pair of hands grasped them both and brought them in. There seemed to be people everywhere and as she gasped for breath she saw that it was Alex bending over Richard.

'Oh, thank God,' she said and turned away to be sick.

'Hannah?'

It was Marge holding her head, she realised dimly, and saying her name urgently. 'Are you all right, Hannah?'

'I'm . . .' Fine, she tried to say, but couldn't quite make it, because suddenly she felt queerer than she'd ever felt in her life. Must be reaction, she thought. I thought he was gone . . . maybe he is? As she tried to push free of Marge, though, Richard stirred beneath Alex's hands and coughed and sat up and then proceeded to relieve himself of a large quantity of creek water.

Hannah felt her chest muscles go loose with relief and when Alex turned to her then, she tried to tell him how glad she was to see him, but that queerly unwell feeling had her in its grip again and she realised she was sweating despite her drenched condition, and she doubled up suddenly in pain.

Both Marge and Alex spoke together, then Alex said sharply, 'What is it, Hannah? Cramp?'

'Yes. No ... I don't know,' she answered with an effort 'Oh ...' she breathed. 'I've never felt like this before ...'

Through a daze of pain she saw Alex glance at Marge's suddenly white face, and something slipped into place in her mind as she herself read the urgent anxiety in Marge's eyes and knew then what was happening to her.

'Oh no!' she gasped. 'Please *no* ...'

'What is it, Marge? Why are you looking like that?' Alex's grim voice interrupted her.

'I think,' Marge hesitated and looked around then lowered her voice to a whisper, 'I think it's the baby. Hannah ...'

'*What?*' The single syllable was uttered in a harsh whisper but it seemed to cut the air.

'Oh!' Marge wrung her hands in despair. 'I thought she must have told you by now. But that's not important right now. The important thing is ...'

Hannah stared bleakly at the wall opposite the bed. It was a high, pristine hospital bed and for the first time in twenty-four hours, she found she could think rationally, though more dismally, than ever before in her life, for the concerted effort the doctors had made to save the baby had failed and she'd miscarried, despite everything, her desperate prayers included.

'There will be others, my dear,' the doctor had said. 'And from what I've been told of the circumstances, you acted with outstanding bravery, so you mustn't reproach yourself ...'

But I do, she thought. Not for saving Richard, never that, but if I'd taken someone down with me perhaps . . . if I'd only stopped to think!

'Hannah?'

She moved convulsively and turned to see Alex standing beside the bed. 'I didn't hear you come in.'

'No.' He pulled up a chair and sat down beside the bed. 'How do you feel?'

'I . . . I don't really know,' she said unhappily. 'All right, I guess.' Her eyes dropped to the sheet bunched in her fingers. 'But I can guess how you feel.' She sniffed and wiped away a tear with the back of her hand.

'Can you?' he said slowly and reached out to tilt her face towards him. 'How do you think I feel?' he said sombrely. 'Tell me.'

She stared at him and it was as if there was a knife twisting in her breast because he looked pale and inexpressibly weary as he'd never looked before and not only, she thought, because he'd been at her side through most of what had happened. She licked her dry lips. 'I . . . I think,' she stammered, 'you must be saying to yourself that you still can't let me out of your sight without me doing something stupid.'

His eyes narrowed and a frown etched itself on his forehead and for about a minute, he didn't say anything, just studied her tear-streaked face.

Then it seemed as if he sighed inwardly and he said quietly and compellingly, 'No, Hannah. You didn't do anything stupid. You saw a life in danger and you saved it—in fact you probably saved two lives because who knows what the other kid might have done. It was a risk you had to take and that wasn't stupid, it was very brave. You could have been drowned yourself.'

'Oh, I don't know about that,' she said awkwardly. 'What I could have done is . . .' She shrugged and twisted away restlessly.

'Hannah,' his voice was suddenly stern and he recaptured her chin and forced her to look at him, 'you couldn't have done anything else. Nobody would have expected you to stand by and let Richard drown. Look, I know I've been angry with you before for things that were ... perhaps ill-judged, but this isn't one of them. It was a risk you had to take and I'm not blaming you for—that.' His voice dropped unexpectedly and for a moment she was shaken by the bleakness she saw in his eyes. Then it was as if he mentally drew a shutter across his thoughts and he said quietly, 'You *mustn't* torment yourself about this.'

'I'm not sorry about Richard,' she said tearfully. 'How could I be? He ... I ... sometimes he reminds me of myself, always in trouble, but if I'd stopped to think I'd have taken someone down with me. I just didn't stop to think!' She scrubbed at her face and took several deep gasping breaths. And if I'd stopped to think, she reminded herself remorselessly, I might not have lost your baby—the most precious thing I ever had.

And possibly, because she felt bone-weary and weaker than she'd thought possible, and incredibly bereft, she found she couldn't stem the flood of tears that rose up within her like a great tide. This time, the feel of his arms around her and his soothing voice didn't comfort her and he reached across and pressed the bell.

She didn't even feel the needle that was administered to her, didn't hear the doctor say to Alex, 'It's a very emotional experience, Mr Cameron, but she'll get over it.'

Neither did she hear Alex say, 'I'd like to stay with her.'

'Of course.'

        ★   ★   ★

It was a week before they let her out of hospital. A week during which she didn't seem to be able to do much, but let life slide along around her. She had plenty of visitors—the Watsons, deeply grateful and particularly concerned for her, Marge and Mick, the Claytons and even Billy Johnson who arrived with a floral tribute he'd actually got from a florist shop. And Alex spent most of his time with her. He never once alluded to what she'd seen in his eyes right after the miscarriage, the bleak registering of the curious fact that she'd never told him about the baby. Yet it was still there, she knew, an unspoken question which she didn't for the life of her know how to answer.

It was also a week during which she turned nineteen and received from Alex a string of pearls.

'Oh! Thank you!' she said in an awed voice, quite stunned by the beauty of them. She raised her eyes shyly to his. 'Thank you—but you shouldn't have.'

He lifted an eyebrow. 'Why not? Don't you like them?'

'I . . . they're beautiful, but much too good for me.'

'Why ever should you say that?' he enquired.

'I don't know,' she confessed.

'Try them on,' he suggested, looking amused. 'They should look good on your skin although they might find their radiance challenged a little.'

She looked at him to see if he was serious and coloured faintly, because she couldn't tell. She said, ruefully, 'My skin doesn't feel very radiant at the moment. Or my hair.' She put a hand to her head and pulled a face. 'Are they ever going to let me out of here?'

He contemplated her up-turned face with its rueful

little smile and something like a sigh seemed to escape him. 'That's better,' he said then. 'I was beginning to think you'd lost interest in . . . everything.'

'N-no,' she said. 'Why did you think that?'

He shrugged again. 'You've been so very quiet and contained.'

It was true, she thought. Since that shattering outburst of weeping, she hadn't shed another tear, just concentrated on getting along from hour to hour.

'I'm sorry,' she said. 'You must have been awfully bored. You've spent so much time here and you must be so . . .'

'Not that,' he interrupted. 'Not bored, but concerned. Now I'm happy to see you . . . coming out of it. Hannah,' he hesitated briefly, 'I don't know if this is the right time to say it but there's no reason, so I'm told, why you couldn't have more babies. Would you like that?'

'Oh yes,' she said slowly, without looking at him. 'But . . .' she shivered, 'I'd have to learn to take better care of them. Oh!' She lifted her eyes as if struck by a sudden thought. 'Do they know? I mean the children—especially Greg? Richard might be too young to understand but Greg . . . and he was supposed to be in charge.'

'They don't know,' he said quietly. 'They think you're in here because you got bruised and battered.'

'I'm so glad,' she said shakily. 'How are they?'

'Missing you.'

'Oh, so am I—missing them,' she said gruffly. 'You didn't . . .' she glanced at him uncertainly, 'I mean, I know Richard shouldn't have done it, but he did have a friend with him and I often think there's a terrible compulsion to show off to one's friends. You didn't . . .?'

'No, I didn't,' he said gently.

She smiled up at him relieved but sobered. 'What about Tom?'

Alex looked faintly amused. 'He didn't either—beyond a severe talking to. You see Richard was absolutely distraught when he discovered you were in hospital and he's spent the most uncomfortable week of his young life I think, worrying about you.' He grinned suddenly. 'I wouldn't go so far as to say he's a reformed character but I shouldn't be surprised if he'll be positively angelic for a while.'

Hannah was silent. Then she said, 'The sooner I get home the better. I have to see this for myself! Could I go today?'

He reached out and ruffled her hair. 'Tomorrow,' he promised.

It was a momentous homecoming. There was a banner strung above the gateposts with WELCOME HOME HANNAH inscribed on it and a party that reminded her of their honeymoon homecoming. There were happy tears shed by several, Hannah included, and Richard kept patting her hand as if to assure himself she was real. Then Alex decided enough was enough and put an early end to this party and insisted Hannah went to bed.

'But I'm fine now,' she protested.

'You do as Alex says!' Marge commanded. 'In fact Sally and I will come up and help you.'

Which decided that and, once she was in bed, Hannah had to admit she was tired. There was a feeling of warmth in her heart too, for the first time since she'd lost the baby, and it seemed to be able to hold at bay a strange sensation that she found hard to describe, a curious feeling of . . . could it be fatalism? she'd wondered. Maybe it's part of the whole experience, she'd told herself, and I'll get over it . . .

The inner warmth continued when Alex came to bed that night and gathered her in his arms and said with a smile just touching his lips, 'I've missed you.'

She relaxed against him with a sigh of relief. 'Me too,' she said in a grave, deep little voice. So much, she thought. A little while later she said sleepily, 'Sometimes we're very good friends, aren't we?'

'Yes,' he agreed and stroked her hair.

'Do you think that's strange, Alex?'

'No. Do you?'

'I don't know. But I'm glad . . .'

'So am I and I hope we'll always be friends,' he said and kissed her gently on the lips. 'What brought this up?' he added gravely.

Hannah tried to concentrate but found it hard with her mind half asleep and her body amazingly soothed by the feel of his next to her. 'I don't know,' she said at last. 'It just comforts me . . .'

He didn't say anything for a long time. Then just as she was on the border of sleep, he spoke. 'I'd do anything to comfort you, Hannah. Didn't you know? I have no choice, my sweet innocent . . .'

His words pierced Hannah's drowsiness for a moment, and she tried valiantly to hold back the cloud of sleep that was enveloping her, because they seemed singularly significant. It seemed supremely important to her, to decipher his meaning, to ask him why he had no choice but the day had taken too great a toll of her still strangely weak body and she fell asleep.

That strange sense of fatalism came back to plague her over the next few weeks. Plus what Alex had said, and she found herself thinking of it often. Why did he have no choice . . .

'Hannah Rosemary Cameron!' Alex's faintly dry

voice interrupted her thoughts one morning, over breakfast.

She looked up. 'I'm sorry! I was miles away—have I done something wrong?'

'Why should you imagine that?' he queried.

'Well, once before you called—well, you called me Hannah Hawthorn actually, after we were married and not . . . I mean, you weren't very happy with me.'

He lifted his eyebrows quizzically. 'It must have slipped out in the heat of the moment. Was I very cross?'

'Very,' Hannah said reminiscently, and shivered slightly as she stared at her cereal bowl and saw instead two yellow eyes. 'But with cause I must admit,' she added ruefully and looked up. 'I guess that's why I wondered if I'd done something . . .'

He regarded her pensively for a moment. Then he said with a shrug, 'No. Unless you can call the degree of preoccupation you exhibit sometimes . . . wrong. But let's not get into that,' he murmured and watched her reaction with narrowed eyes, as if he was testing her somehow.

Of course, it's still there, she thought with a sense of panic. It's not gone away just because he's been so nice to me while I recuperate. That unspoken question is still there and still unanswered . . .

She stared at him with her lips parted, but her mind stupidly, refusing to function.

Until something very like impatience flickered briefly in his eyes before he looked down and said evenly, 'I was only trying to tell you that we shall be having company for dinner tonight. Alison Wandsworth. She's expressed a desire to meet you and I think you'll like her. She's also rather lonely at the moment, as you can probably imagine.'

Hannah swallowed. 'Oh. Yes. Yes I can . . .'

CHAPTER EIGHT

MRS Hunter fairly quivered with excitement when Hannah imparted the news to her after breakfast.

'Oh my,' she said. 'Fancy that! I wondered if he'd bring her here ... I mean,' she amended hastily and guiltily, 'well, it so happens I have a cousin who used to work for her and she reckoned that everything was done absolutely *beautifully* up there!'

Hannah regarded Mrs Hunter steadily for a moment, then she said quietly, 'I think we do things rather nicely ourselves. But let's ...' She hesitated briefly, for so far she'd tried not to impinge too greatly on Mrs Hunter's domain, but, she thought suddenly, she has as much tact as a ... as a ... so why should I bother ...

'What?' Mrs Hunter asked.

'I was going to say, let's really let ourselves go. I've got some gorgeous recipes.'

Mrs Hunter started to look faintly put out. Then, surprisingly, her face creased into a smile. 'Why not?' she said. 'We'll show 'em.'

Later she said with grudging admiration, 'I had no idea you were such a good cook, Hannah! You should have told me.'

'I haven't had that much practice. It might be beginner's luck.'

'Well, I don't know about that. Your pastry is so light ... Now,' she looked around, 'I think we've done everything we can do. The Avocado Ritz is ready to be served, the Coral Trout is dressed and ready to be baked and the sauce to go with it is ready and just needs reheating. I was lucky to find that Coral Trout, they're not that easy to come by! And the apricot sorbet is made and the fruit pie. Cream—cream,' she said rapidly and looked around. 'Don't tell me I forgot to get the cream! But I'm sure . . .'

'You didn't forget,' Hannah said soothingly. 'It's whipped and in the fridge.'

'Oh, of course. Right!' She glanced at her watch. 'And we're well ahead of schedule so while I whip round the house and make sure it glows, why don't you go up and lie down?'

'I . . .'

'Now you just do as I tell you, Hannah,' Mrs Hunter said crossly. 'If Alex was here he'd tell you to do it and you wouldn't argue with him. After all it's not so long since you lost your baby.'

Hannah winced inwardly and wondered if she'd ever lose that shaft of pain that pierced her heart at the thought of what she'd lost. She fell asleep thinking of it . . .

She woke about an hour later to find the last rays of sunshine bathing the room in gold, and the scent of orange blossom strong on the air. She lay for a time, feeling the slow flicker of panic at the pit of her stomach at the prospect of the evening that lay ahead.

Then, for no reason at all, she thought of her beloved father in the strange context that he too had lost a loved one, and she found it strangely comforting.

She took her time choosing her clothes from the now greatly extended wardrobe she possessed, and finally settled on a sleeveless dress of grey, silky polyester with small shadowy checks of lilac and green on it. It had a narrow, stand-up collar trimmed with a discreet frill and a similar frill on the yoke, and it had a wide, soft, silver belt to go with it.

It was the first time she had worn it, and she studied her reflection carefully in the mirror and liked what she saw. The silver belt emphasised the smallness of her waist and the muted colours seemed to make her skin look luminous, her eyes all grey and her hair very dark as it lay thick and smooth, in a shining cap. She reached for Alex's gift and noted with pleasure that the long strand of evenly matched pearls looked beautiful against the grey and subtle shading of lilac and green. A pair of high-heeled silver sandals completed the outfit.

She tilted her head to one side and murmured out aloud, 'Not bad. I just wish I looked a little . . .'

'As a matter of fact you look lovely,' a voice interrupted from behind her, and she turned with her heart in her mouth and a faint tinge of colour in her cheeks to see Alex lounging in the doorway. 'What do you wish?' he asked, not quite smiling at her.

'Nothing,' she said hastily, although she'd been going to say 'older'. 'I didn't hear you come home,' she added embarrassedly.

He straightened up and strolled across the room to where she stood. 'We chose well when we chose this, didn't we?' he said lightly and fingered the frill on the yoke, and then the pearls and finally looked up.

Hannah caught her breath at the expression in his eyes. She'd seen it before, on their wedding night, on the beach that day in Zanzibar and other times. But not since the night he'd taken her in anger and forced a response from her that still made her go hot and cold to think of it. That had been at the back of most of her fears, she realised. The fact that she'd disappointed him that night; that she'd been so stunned afterwards, so . . . well, perhaps immature about it, whereas Alison Wandsworth could not be classed as immature, she was quite sure . . .

Before she had time to respond to that look in his eyes, only to wonder if she was imagining it, he turned away and started to unbutton his shirt, and he said casually, 'I need a shower but I won't be long. Why don't you go down and make us two cool drinks?' And he disappeared into the bathroom.

She went downstairs slowly, all of a sudden supremely uncertain again. Then, with a sigh, she forced herself to take hold and concentrate on the task ahead and to call on every ounce of poise that had been drummed into her with more wisdom perhaps, than she'd realised at the time . . .

'Now that was absolutely delicious!' Alison Wandsworth said with a sigh of pleasure and a warm, warm smile. 'To whom . . .' she glanced from Mrs Hunter who was clearing the plates, to Hannah, 'should I pay respects for that magnificently prepared and served Coral Trout? Or was it a team effort?'

'Yes . . .' Hannah said, but Mrs Hunter immediately contradicted her. 'No, ma'am,' she said. 'I have to confess it was all Hannah's idea and just about all her work. And you haven't had the last of it, her dessert is just as good!'

'Now that,' Alex said as the door closed behind Mrs Hunter, 'is praise indeed, Hannah. To have impressed Alison is one thing but to have impressed Mrs Hunter and what's more, have her admit it willingly, is another thing altogether!'

'Oh dear!' Alison laughed and her perfect white teeth shone. 'Like that is she, our Mrs Hunter?'

'Well,' Hannah said, with a faint grin herself, 'no, not really. It's, well it's hard to explain.' She shrugged.

Alex said, 'Hannah is being modest. She has a rare talent for getting through to people.'

'I can believe it,' Alison said quietly and very sincerely. 'It's been a pleasure to meet you, my dear.'

'You too,' Hannah said and hoped her voice didn't sound as shaken as she felt, because she'd spoken the truth. She had not known what to expect of her feelings when she finally met this woman, but to find herself really liking her had shaken her ... Alison was not only gorgeous, but she was also warm and friendly and she had a way of making it impossible not to be at ease in her company.

Or almost at ease, Hannah thought later as they sat on the terrace with their coffee and she found herself studying their guest obliquely. She was nearly as tall as Alex and still as slender as a girl and her skin was clear and beautiful and her eyes faintly green in certain lights. But it was more, much more ... She had a sort of vital radiance about her, an aura of intelligence, but then just occasionally it was as if she lowered her guard and there was a haunting sadness in her eyes that touched your heart strings.

Is that why I don't feel quite at ease? Hannah wondered. Because there's been nothing else—no *sign* that they might be still in love, nothing to make me feel uncomfortable or embarrassed, nothing ...

Then her whole world came crashing down.

She'd gone to make a last cup of coffee, having sent Mrs Hunter off duty after dinner, and she'd come back almost immediately and silently across the darkened lounge to suggest that they have Irish coffee. But two words had stopped her in her tracks just inside the french windows, hidden by the long curtains.

'Oh, Alex!' Alison said softly, but despairingly.

Hannah froze.

'To think that we wasted—at least I wasted so much time and it's . . . turned out like this.'

'I know.' Alex's voice was quiet and strained. 'I'm *sorry* . . .'

'Don't be. You mustn't be. No one could have known . . . Let's talk about Hannah instead. She's lovely and so sweet and . . .'

No.

Hannah put her hands over her ears and turned swiftly to go back the way she'd come. No, let's not talk about Hannah, she said to herself. I couldn't bear that because if it wasn't for Hannah . . .

She stopped just inside the kitchen door and leant back against it with her heart pounding and a strange, ringing sensation in her ears. Oh God, she prayed, oh no! I don't *want* to believe it now but . . . what was it Marge said? I said something about proof and she said when it hits you on the head . . . And now it has!

'But I think I knew it always would,' she whispered to herself and felt hot tears on her cheeks. 'It was like a feeling of . . . fate, especially when I lost the baby. Yes, I think I knew then . . . Knew then that I had a choice. That I could no longer *pretend* to myself that I had no choice where Alex was concerned . . .'

'Are you all right, Hannah?' Alex said with a slight frown when she finally reappeared with the coffee.

'Fine! Sorry I took so long. Did you think I'd gone to Brazil for the beans?'

For weeks afterwards, Hannah marvelled at how easy

it had been to leave Alex once she'd made the decision—as if it had been fate too, and as if with so much fate on her side, it had to be the right thing to have done. For example, with the decision made but no idea of how to implement it, she'd been glancing though the positions vacant column of the paper and come across an entry that read ... Desperate mother of three requires nanny-cum-governess in a temporary capacity. Children aged from three to eight—fourth on the way. We are in an isolated outback area but successful applicant would be treated like one of the family. Ring Cairns area code and reverse charges ...

Hannah had rung and got the job. The resident nanny had had to leave the Clarke family unexpectedly for a time, because of an illness in her family and, on the same day, Mrs Clarke had severely sprained her ankle and to make matters worse, the father of the family was urgently engaged on a muster before the Wet season began in earnest. They would need someone for about three months and—another stroke of fate—had heard of Hannah's father so were more than happy to have her ...

Hannah had arranged to fly to Cairns where the Clarkes would have a lift set up for her for the journey inland. All that had remained was for her to go. Which she'd done—slipped away in a horse transporter that had delivered a consignment of horses for the Wandsworth auction and got a lift into town. It hadn't been quite as simple as that, though, because she could only think of the letter she'd left and the lies she'd told and had discovered that all she felt like doing was crawling into a hole and dying ...

Twenty-four hours later, she was looking out of the window of a giant juggernaut bound for the Gulf Country that was to drop her off at the Clarke property. All she had with her were her own clothes and all she had to remind her of her marriage was her wedding ring strung on a slender chain around her neck and a packet of photographs of their honeymoon. Even as she sat and stared at the lush cane-fields around her, living proof that she was now in Far North Queensland, over a thousand miles away from Alex, she couldn't quite believe what she'd done. Nor could she in any way rid her heart and soul of the terrible pain of it, indeed she doubted if she ever would.

I'll have to learn to stop crying every time I think of him, she told herself distractedly and sniffed, so that the truckie turned to her and gave her an understanding smile. 'I think you're a long way from home, kid,' he said kindly. 'But I'll tell you what. The Clarkes are real kind hearted folks and they'll be good to you—that I can guarantee.'

He wasn't wrong, Hannah discovered. Mary Clarke was voluble and warm and before very long, was treating Hannah just as the advertisement said, as one of the family. And she certainly needed Hannah, being still confined to crutches as well as heavily pregnant.

While Hannah fitted in so well, she couldn't, for a time, however, rid herself of the secret hope that Alex might somehow track her down and arrive to claim her. She even dreamt about it and dreamt of him denying he had ever loved Alison Fairleigh and that it had all been a misunderstanding. Then, even that secret hope wilted and died as the days passed, and all she had left were her memories.

She lost weight, much to her employer's concern and couldn't seem to lose the faintly blue shadows beneath her eyes, but just when Mary Clarke had decided to tackle her new governess and find out what it was she had run away from—Hannah had no idea she was so transparent—an event occured which precipitated a flurry of panic.

In fact it started as Mary was watching Hannah read a bedtime story to the children. So young, so lovely and so sad! Mary mused to herself as she let the baby dress she was embroidering, rest in her lap. And so determined not to let on, but she's been an absolute tower of strength to me and that's all the more reason for me to get to the bottom of it ... Why that's strange, she thought, and moved restlessly and immediately forgot Hannah. I've still got weeks to go, and I never have my babies early ...

However, as it turned out, this Clarke baby was in a particular hurry to enter the world and was not to be deterred about it. The night suddenly became one neither Mary nor Hannah would ever forget.

Hannah certainly knew she'd never forget the feeling at the pit of her stomach once she'd taken stock of the situation and realised what she'd have to do. She'd managed to contact Ray Clarke on the two-way radio—he was out in the blue yonder, completing the muster and had just struck camp for the night, which he hastily unstruck, but told Hannah he had a three to four hour drive to get home. The nearest neighbour was at least that distance away too, she knew, and for a variety of reasons, she discovered, the Flying Doctor Service would not be able to reach the homestead for hours either ...

'We can patch you through to a doctor, though,' a reassuring voice said to her over the airwaves. 'The important thing is not to panic. These things usually take time and anyway, Mary's an old hand at this.'

Thank God! Hannah thought but said doubtfully, 'I don't think this is going to take that long. Neither does Mary ...'

'Then we'll be with you every step of the way,' the disembodied voice said soothingly.

Indeed, Mary's two chief concerns seemed to be that the children would be frightened, and what she was putting Hannah through.

Hannah looked down at her affectionately, noting the beading of sweat on her upper lip. Taking a deep breath, she said with a little smile, 'If you can get through this, so can I. It's the least I can do. And I just checked on the children and they're fast asleep.'

'Ray wanted me to go to Cairns for the last month,' Mary said fretfully, 'but I thought if I went a week beforehand I'd be in plenty of time . . . oh!' She clutched the side of the bed, grimaced and then lay back with a shuddering sigh.

'Don't worry about it now,' Hannah said gently. 'We've more urgent things to do!' She bathed Mary's face with a damp cloth and was surprised to realise how calm she was feeling now. Then she went back to the radio to give the doctor on the other end as accurate a picture as she could of Mary's condition, to receive his considered opinion that the birth was a good few hours away yet and that help would probably arrive in time.

But, as Mary said with a wry smile, doctors were known to be wrong and exactly one hour later, Hannah wiped the sweat off her own face and said, in a voice that trembled with awe, 'It's a boy and he's a beauty. Now all I have to . . . oh no,' she added, as the baby began to cry, 'he's done it all by himself . . .'

'A boy!' Mary said delightedly. 'That'll even things up. Oh, thank you, Hannah . . .'

'Don't thank me,' Hannah said and they were both laughing and crying at the same time, 'you did all the work. But we still have to deal with the cord.'

She found she felt strangely weak then, as she listened to the doctor's measured instructions. 'Got that, Hannah?' he asked. 'I'll go through it again if you like.'

'Yes please,' Hannah said. 'I think ... I don't know but I don't feel quite as ... as ...'

'I know what you mean. It's reaction. But you did a marvellous job, Hannah, by the sound of it. Now ...'

And ten minutes later she laid the baby beside Mary. 'There. Isn't he beautiful? Look at those plump cheeks. I think you make good babies, Mary.'

Mary looked and agreed. 'What shall we call him? If he was a girl I'd call him Hannah but ... anyway, you choose. Please.'

'I ... do you really want me to?'

'Dear Hannah, yes!'

'Then, if you like the names, William Alexander, that's what I would choose,' Hannah said. 'William after my father and Alex after ... I mean, I like that name.'

'That's what he'll be called then ... oh! Listen to that!' Mary said, with a weary grin. 'Sounds like a plane.'

It was, but because Mary was fine and the baby perfectly healthy it was decided not to transfer her to the Cairns Base Hospital, especially as she had Hannah to help out at home.

So it was, that the last few weeks of Hannah's stay with the Clarkes had another form of torment added to it. William Alexander Clarke was christened with Hannah as godmother, and throve on his mother's and Hannah's care. Every time she held him, though, Hannah felt that terrible ache in her heart at the thought of what she'd lost; and other thoughts too, like the one that if her own baby had been a boy she'd

have called him William Alexander and the rock
bottom thought that she probably never would have a
baby now because, without Alex to give her one, there
would never be anyone she could put in his place in
her life or her heart.

Mary came up with a surprise at the end of
Hannah's stay. She had searched her heart and
decided that if Hannah didn't want to share her
problems, it wasn't her place to barge in. Which didn't
mean she couldn't do as much for Hannah as possible,
however, and after discreetly enquiring whether
Hannah had any immediate plans, made a suggestion.

'We have a cottage on the beach near Mossman. It's
nothing grand but it's so beautiful up there, it's the
perfect place to relax and have a holiday and that's
what Ray and I would like you to do for as long as you
like.'

Hannah, who was folding nappies, stopped and
stared at her employer. 'I . . .' she said at last, 'I really
can't think of anything I'd rather do. But . . .'

'No buts,' Mary said firmly. 'It's settled. Ray will
arrange a lift for you and we'll provide the provisions
so you won't have to worry. There's a freezer in the
place. There's just one thing, though,' she added,
fondly, 'don't you dare not keep in touch with us,
Hannah!'

'Well, if you think I'd do that to a godchild of mine,'
Hannah said in mock reproach, but relented immediately and crossed the room to kiss Mary warmly.
'Thank you,' she said and blinked away a tear.
'Talking of whom,' she went on, 'I think I hear him
stirring. And since he's slept for four hours straight, I
imagine he'll be very cross and hungry in a minute!'

Mary grinned ruefully. 'You wouldn't be wrong!'

★   ★   ★

'Hannah!'

Hannah froze, then looked about her incredulously. The main street of Cairns was bright with colour and movement and the clear day was very hot. Her lift, another juggernaut bound for Cooktown this time, was at present taking on supplies at a warehouse and she had an hour to kill before they embarked on the Cairns-Mossman leg of the trip.

'Hannah!'

Her name came again from across the wide busy street and a moment later the Reverend Clayton sprinted into view dodging the traffic with careless disregard for life and limb.

She sucked in a breath, then he was beside her on the pavement and his first words to her were, 'I ought to shake the living daylights out of you, Hannah Hawthorn! Where have you been? And why?'

His normally placid blue eyes sparkled furiously at her and he did in fact take her by the shoulders, but, as her face paled, he forced himself to relax and he folded her into a wide, warm embrace. 'Oh, you silly, foolish child,' he said softly. 'I'm so glad to see you!'

'So am I,' Hannah wept into his shoulder to the intense interest of all the passers-by.

'There, there,' he murmured, 'don't cry. Come.' He released her and took her by the hand and led her into a nearby coffee shop.

'And that's why I did it,' Hannah said, two reviving cups of coffee later. 'Don't you see . . .'

'Well, my dear,' Ted Clayton interrupted, 'I do see, but I can't applaud it. You've put all of us through hell, Alex included.'

'But . . .'

'Hannah,' he interrupted, 'I . . . well, I can't believe,

whether he's in love with this other woman or not, that he would be happy to think of you alone in the world.'

'I . . . in the letter I left,' Hannah said hesitantly, 'I more or less said I was tired of being married, that I wanted to be free again, to see the world and so on. He couldn't blame himself for that, you see. I thought it would leave the way open for them, so that when twelve months is up, they can go ahead with a clear conscience. I said I'd get in touch through a solicitor then to arrange the divorce. I also said,' her voice shook, 'that I'd thought I'd loved him but discovered it was that I'd been . . . dazzled and so on, and probably too young to know my own mind at the time. I just couldn't think of any other way to do it,' she whispered and stared blindly down at the table. 'If he really knew how I felt about him, he'd never let me go—he's not that sort of person, but I found I couldn't bear the thought of him being chained to me when his heart was elsewhere. Oh!' she pleaded, looking up. 'Please say you understand.'

Ted Clayton frowned and sighed and thought he'd give his right arm *to* understand. 'In a way,' he said. 'If what you overheard is true. But I must confess he looked quite demented when he came to see me. Which I didn't help, I'm afraid . . . And I know he flew all over the place looking for you.'

Hannah said with a sad little smile, 'That's because he doesn't think I can take care of myself. But I have quite well, haven't I?'

He looked at her, noting the weight she'd lost and those faint blue shadows beneath her eyes, and he started to say something, but changed his mind and said instead, 'And you always knew about this woman, Hannah?'

'Yes. That's why I knew he married me for . . . well, other reasons.'

'Then you misled me, Hannah.'

'I know. But not really. I mean it was what I wanted to do.'

'I had a feeling something was wrong,' Ted Clayton said reminiscently. 'I have to tell you, my dear, that when Alex came to see me—only hours after you had left, I behaved in a rather unpriestly way. In fact I called the wrath of God down on his head in no uncertain terms, and I accused him of mistreating you.'

'But he *didn't* . . .'

'Well—and you say he didn't know that *you* knew about this woman?'

'No. There was no way he could unless . . .' She stopped abruptly and wondered for the first time what Marge Riley would have done after she'd left. How awkward would it have been for Marge, though? Very awkward . . . 'No he didn't know at the time, and I doubt if he does now,' she said.

The Reverend Clayton was silent for some time, and unbeknownst to Hannah, was in fact grappling with his conscience and his peculiarly ambivalent feelings towards Alex Cameron. Then he said slowly and perhaps a little unwillingly, 'My dear, you should go back to him. No, let me finish, it's not only because I don't believe in divorce except in extreme circumstances, but all my life I've believed that honesty is the best policy. So while I understand something of your dilemma and appreciate your motives, I think that's what you should do—go back and lay your cards on the table. You knew this marriage would be difficult—for that matter, most marriages are—but it was never intended to be a state as easily backed out of as you are trying to, I believe. I'm *sorry*,' he added as Hannah flinched, 'but I think you owe it to him anyway, my dear.'

'If ... if you could put yourself in my place, though. Once I'm honest with him, he'll never let me go. How would you feel?'

Ted Clayton grimaced. 'You're not going to like me for this, but I think, whatever you feel, you're his wife and you should carry on being that.'

'And hope that in the fullness of time,' she said wearily, 'he falls in love with me and forgets her.'

'It's happened. Besides, it would seem he—cares greatly about you . . .'

'I know he loves me in a way,' Hannah said unhappily. 'Because I'm my father's daughter mainly. Have you seen him lately?' she asked huskily.

'No. I . . . well, I told you how I felt. I believe Mrs Clayton keeps in touch though,' he added a little stiffly, for the truth of the matter was that he and Mrs Clayton had had a major argument too, over his treatment of Alex, and they now preserved a slightly chilly silence on the subject. Dear me! he thought suddenly, what an argumentative, unforgiving person I've become. Perhaps it's time I started practising what I preach . . .

'Will you tell him you've met me?'

Hannah's words pierced his abstraction and he frowned. 'I—hadn't thought of it. No, I think I might leave it up to you. What are you doing in Cairns by the way?'

She told him then smiled faintly. 'I was going to ask you the same question.'

'I'm on my way to Thursday Island to assist with the opening of a new church.'

There was a suddenly tense little silence, tense for

Hannah at least, as she thought of her dear friend and mentor's earlier words—I'll leave that up to you. And she knew he was still waiting for an answer. 'I . . . I'll try,' she said. 'I'll think about it . . .'

'Good,' he replied. 'I have great faith in you, Hannah, I know you'll find the courage to do the right thing.'

She flinched. 'That's hitting below the belt,' she murmured. 'I just don't know if I have that kind of courage. I will think about it, though, I promise. And thank you for not . . . treating me like a child.'

'Ah, but I'm not letting you walk out of here without extracting another kind of promise from you! And that's that you keep in touch with Mrs Clayton and myself *whatever*.'

'I promise I will,' Hannah said tearfully. 'I really do.' She glanced at her watch and jumped. 'Oh! I'm almost late . . .'

Several minutes later, the Reverend Clayton watched her weave her way through the tables and walk out into the bright hot sunshine, and he sighed heavily.

Did I do the right thing? he asked himself. Should I have let her slip away? But I sincerely believe she has to make the decision herself. I gave her the right advice. I did do that in spite of my . . . fatherly feelings. I put on my other cap, so to speak.

He stared in front of him and didn't see the salt and pepper shakers or the sugar jug with its silver spout on top that was supposed to dispense the sugar out teaspoon by teaspoon but rarely did. Instead he saw Mrs Clayton and her calm eyes and he thought suddenly of forsaking the new church on Thursday Island because it seemed to him the last thing he should be doing when he was in discord with her . .

Some say love ... is a very tricky business, he mused. And here was I preaching reconciliation when ... but we were both right. I was right to be worried and you were right about how vulnerable to her conscience Hannah was. So what say I ring you up and say I love you very much even although I can be stubborn and argumentative, all the things I shouldn't be? And he reached into his pocket and pulled out all his twenty cent pieces ...

CHAPTER NINE

It took six days of the incredible peace and beauty of Mossman for Hannah to come to a decision.

The cottage was in a secluded spot and she saw no one and was grateful for it, because it only dawned on her, among the tranquillity of the tropical garden with its steps down to the beach, how tired she was. She slept for hours during the day as well as the night. She swam in the early morning when the sea was a pale aquamarine, and in the late afternoon when the heat of the day was still heavy on the land. She also shamelessly plundered the giant mango tree and sat for hours beneath its thick, protective foliage, staring out to sea or drinking in the scenery and the magic of the coastline.

I could live here, she thought more than once. If I could find a way to make a living, I could live here for ever. Perhaps I could find a job in the town? But then I couldn't expect to live in the cottage for ever.

These were the kind of thoughts that came, she found. And thoughts about the relatively slender state of her finances, but thinking of Alex was what she couldn't do, despite her promise.

Then on the sixth day that problem was solved for her in an unexpected way—all her problems were.

She'd dropped a note to Mary Clarke to let her know she'd arrived safely and five days later she received a long, newsy letter in reply, full of the latest doings of Master William Alexander Clarke and his brothers and sisters. But the surprising bit had come after that—an offer of a job as secretary-companion to a friend of Mary Clarke's who actually lived in Mossman.

'. . . Fay and I went to school together,' Hannah read, 'and we've kept in touch ever since. You might have heard of her, she writes children's books and she's quite famous for it. Anyhow, she drove in to see me the day you left, to see William and, to cut a long story short, mentioned that she was looking for someone to work for her. I thought of you straight away because I remembered you saying you could type and so on, and when I told her about you she got quite excited. Of course, the final decision is up to the two of you, but knowing her and knowing you, I could imagine you getting along like a house on fire. Of course again, if you've made other plans, Hannah . . .' Hannah's eyes skimmed a couple of lines and came back to the salient points—Fay Carlisle would be back in Mossman in a fortnight's time after a trip to Sydney and would be very happy to meet Hannah.

She let the letter fall to her lap and stared out over the ocean abstractedly. It sounded perfect, she thought with a shiver of sadness. The perfect answer for what was an imperfect life from the day she'd left Alex . . .

All of a sudden, as if some inner floodgates had opened, she found herself thinking of Alex, and the Reverend Ted's advice. Thinking and trying to assess everything critically and dispassionately for the first time. To find in the end that there was only one answer . . . The same answer. The answer that left her with tears streaming down her cheeks as she sat through the sunset not seeing it, and not hearing the flock of white cockatoos that made a daily visit to the garden each late afternoon before wheeling away in a noisy squawking crowd.

She sat on until it was quite dark and an impudent possum who lived in the roof was fooled into thinking his domain was no longer occupied, and skittered across the verandah only a foot or so away from her.

The moon rose. A full moon, a great golden orb that stretched a pale path of radiance across the water, but still she didn't stir, or see in its light the ghostly, black-winged flying foxes that flitted silently around the garden before settling in the mango tree and she didn't hear their occasional bickering chitters as they squabbled for their upside down positions.

Finally an alien sound did intrude into her numb sense of isolation. Possibly because it was totally alien, for there was no reason why a car should stop at the garden gate. The cottage was the only house at the end of a stretch of dirt road. She felt a flicker of apprehension as she turned her head at the sound of it and saw the headlights doused and the interior light flick on as the driver's door opened . . .

Then she was on her feet but clutching the verandah table for support and her heart was beating like a drum and her mouth dry. It can't be, she thought wildly.

But it was. There was no mistaking that tall figure coming unhurriedly down the garden path, no hope that the moonlight was playing tricks on her or that she was dreaming.

And all she could do was stand there, still foolishly clutching the table for support until he was right in front of her, standing there and looking down at her . . .

She swallowed again and said weakly, breathlessly, 'Alex . . .?'

'Hello, Hannah.'

'H-how . . . did you find me? Did he . . . but he said he wouldn't.'

He raised his eyebrows. 'Is that all you're worried about? How I found you?' he asked drily. 'Well, I'll tell you. I happened to be reading a copy of Country Life yesterday and in it there was a story about a Mrs Mary Clarke whose baby had arrived early and been delivered by the governess ... Who, it went on to say, was well known throughout the Outback as the daughter of the Reverend William Hawthorn ... what did you say?' he enquired as Hannah made an inarticulate sound.

'Nothing,' she whispered. 'Please, don't be angry with me but ...'

'Angry?' he interrupted. 'I think that's putting it mildly. '*Don't* do that,' he warned, as she tried to turn away, and took her chin in his fingers. 'I could kill you, Hannah, for doing what you did,' he said very softly. 'I've scoured the length and breadth of Queensland—and further afield, looking for you and I must tell you, if you ever do it again, I'll put you over my knee and beat the living daylights out of you. Do you understand?'

She stared up at him, her grey eyes wide and frightened but also amazingly stubborn. 'No,' she said stiffly. 'I don't. You can't force me to stay married to you if I don't want to. And if you think beating the living daylights out of me will make me change my mind, you're mistaken. I'm *sorry* I put you to so much trouble, but if you'd just for once, thought of me as an adult, you'd have realised I could take care of myself and you needn't have gone to all that trouble. Nor would you threaten me like you've just done as if I was a kid still in school. So you can just go away again,' she said scornfully.

Despite her brave words, though, she felt her heartbeat trip at the sudden flash of fury she saw in his eyes.

Then it was gone and he said quite gently, 'Oh? Then I'll have to find another way to do it, won't I? And I agree,' he murmured, 'a much more pleasant way of going about things ...' He released her chin and his eyes roamed her face as her lips parted with stunned, incredulous anger.

She tried to speak but found she couldn't and he smiled faintly, but it wasn't a pleasant smile, and his voice was mocking as he said, 'And I'd do it, Hannah, whether you wanted me to or not, but, in point of fact, it shouldn't be too hard to make you want it. That was never too hard, even when you were angry with me, if I recall.' He looked at her lips consideringly and then glanced significantly down the length of her body and if he'd used his hands, she felt, with a hot blushing sense of shame, that he could hardly have undressed her more effectively.

What was worse, was that in the bright moonlight he saw the colour pour into her face, and he laughed at her confusion and consternation.

'Oh!' she breathed, suddenly gloriously and violently angry. 'You seem to think you own me! But you don't ...'

'Try to run away again and you might find differently,' he said flatly. 'And now ...' He glanced at the luminous dial of his watch.

'No!' she cried. 'Now nothing! I'm not going home with you now or ever.'

He looked at her cynically. 'That wasn't what I had in mind just yet. I was wondering if you might offer me something to eat—I seemed to have missed out on most meals today. And I was going to suggest you might like to calm down and discuss this with me ...' He paused and stared at her searchingly.

Hannah was riding high on a terrible sense of

injustice that quite wiped out any other emotion. 'There's nothing to discuss,' she flashed at him. 'I . . . I hate you and despise you and the best thing I ever did was run away from you. I . . .' She stopped abruptly and took a step backwards as he moved then. 'Alex,' she said in a different voice, low and shaken. 'No . . .'

'Yes, Hannah,' he said very quietly. 'Don't fight me.'

But she did. She tried to turn and run from him but stumbled and felt his arms round her. 'No,' she sobbed and twisted and turned but he picked her up and looked around. Yet once inside the cottage he didn't bother to look for the bedroom but deposited her on the broad, soft settee in the lounge that led off the verandah.

She caught her breath and moved precipitously, but he merely sat down beside her and pinned her to the settee with his hands on her shoulders. Nothing she could do broke his grip, until tears of frustration welled up and slid down her cheeks despite a fierce resolve not to give him the satisfaction of making her cry.

She went limp suddenly and bit her lip and shut her eyes, because she couldn't bear to see him gazing down at her sombrely and with a nerve beating in his jaw and know that she had nothing to fight him with. But fight what? she thought desolately as she felt his fingers on the buttons of her blouse that she wore with a simple cotton skirt. Maybe that's why I can't find the weapons to use because I don't really want to fight him at all? At least I did. Until a minute ago I *did*. Oh . . . don't do this to me, Alex!

Her eyes flew open as she felt his fingers trail across her breasts unhindered, because she wasn't wearing a bra. And she said aloud what she'd said to herself, 'Please don't do it to me this way—again.' She stared up at him, her eyes wide and shimmering with tears. 'Please don't,' she whispered. 'I . . .' But she found she couldn't go on.

He gazed down at her for a long time and she got the queer feeling that the sight of the pale, naked skin of her breasts and the golden sheen of her shoulders, hurt him in some inexplicable way.

Then his eyes lifted to hers and his hands moved but to draw her blouse together, and he said, 'All right. I won't do it this way if you can tell me now, and convince me, that everything you wrote in that letter was the truth. Can you, Hannah?'

She went totally still beneath his hands and they stared deep into each other's eyes. Then she took a long, shuddering breath and thought strangely that this must be like drowning. At least, what she'd read of it and how you experienced flashbacks of your life— vivid mental pictures of being stuck in a lift, being rescued from the Southport Police station, a little girl fallen off her bike and a rain-sodden night . . . the fragrance of orange blossom and Africa—oh, Africa, and an angry lioness and being called Missy Mama and being loved—in a way.

'No,' she whispered. 'I can't.'

'Why not?'

'Because I . . .' she swallowed, 'I lied. I'm sorry, but I thought it was for the best. And it was,' she said huskily, and a pulse beat steadily in her throat as she stared up at the ceiling.

He said, 'No, Hannah.' His voice was uneven and his hands moved gently on her.

'Yes,' she answered bleakly and looked at him. How can I make him understand? she wondered torturedly.

Perhaps the Reverend Ted was right and only truth will do?

She lifted a hand involuntarily and touched his face and took a deep breath. 'You see I . . . I knew about you and Alison Fairleigh. Oh, it wasn't anyone's fault but when she came back I . . . well, I thought it was best for you and her, but now I know it was best for *me*, really. I just couldn't bear to play second fiddle. You might,' she hesitated, 'you might think that sounds pretentious and I know the Reverend Ted thinks I should have buried those thoughts and tried to be a good little wife—but I can't. I don't think I could have even if Alison hadn't come back. I . . . I didn't realise that until just now,' she said wonderingly, and then grimaced almost immediately. 'Is that pride? I don't know. It's supposed to be a sin but . . . I think to you, I'll always be the daughter of a dear friend, a kid who gets herself into trouble often, not a soulmate. That's what I can't live with.'

Something like a smile twisted his lips. 'You'll always be those things to me. I can't change that but . . .'

'Then,' she interrupted him tensely, trying desperately to put her soul into words, 'do you see why I can't come back? Please say you do! And . . . and we could still be friends,' she said with an effort, 'if you wanted to. We once agreed we were good friends. I think that's what we were meant to be, not . . . lovers.' Oh God, she thought, would I have the strength to do it this way? But perhaps it's the one way he'll let me go.

He said after a moment, 'Hannah, there's one thing you don't understand.'

She tried not to wince as he smoothed her hair. 'Yes I do,' she whispered as he didn't go on immediately. 'I know what you're going to say. You think because you were the first one to make love to me, that I'll . . . that I'll be scarred for the rest of my life because we didn't . . . because . . .' She drew a breath and sought for the right words.

'Wouldn't you?' he asked and slid his arm round her to draw her on to his lap.

'N-no,' she said but hid her face in his shoulder.

'Well I would,' he said, and stilled her urgent movement with his hands. 'Because you see, I couldn't bear the thought of not having the right to make love to you. Nor could I live with the thought of someone else making love to you. I never could. I found that out, one night in a blaze of anger. Which was why I . . . made love to you that first time when I shouldn't have—so that you'd have to marry me. Because I knew then that I had to have sole, exclusive rights to Hannah Hawthorn in bed and out of it . . .'

His dark gaze rested lingeringly on her lips which had parted in stunned surprise, then moved to her wide, dazed eyes and he smiled, a slight smile full of inwardly directed mockery. 'And that's why you have to come back to me, you see, Missy Mama. Did you never even suspect it?'

Hannah lay transfixed in his arms. He traced the outline of her mouth with one finger and said a little wryly, 'Don't look so shocked . . .'

'I . . .' she licked her lips, 'I . . . but why didn't you tell me? And about—I mean, about Alison. I *heard* . . .' She broke off as she saw something change in his eyes, a sudden alertness come to them and she tensed as he spoke.

'So you did hear something?'

She nodded miserably. 'It wasn't that I was deliberately eavesdropping,' she said tearfully. 'I'd only come back to ask if you'd like Irish coffee . . .'

'And Marge *was* right,' he said almost to himself. 'What a fool I was.' He lifted his head and stared across the room unseeingly. Then he looked down at her and said steadily, 'You misunderstood what you heard, Hannah. No,' he put a finger to her lips, 'it wasn't your fault. It was mine—although Marge feels dreadfully guilty, but she wasn't to know. In a way, that was my problem too. You see I had no idea you'd ever heard of Alison Fairleigh.' His lips twisted. 'In fact I had no idea Alison and I had provided so much food for gossip for so long. Otherwise I would have said something.' He grimaced. 'Perhaps I should have said something anyway.'

'. . . Then, it wasn't true? The . . . the gossip?' Hannah said haltingly, and thought—this must be a dream, I shall wake up shortly.

'Oh, it was true,' he said drily and Hannah licked her lips. Here it comes . . . 'We fell in love,' he went on. 'What the gossips didn't know, though, was that we fell out of love too. Perhaps it wasn't the real thing in the first place, although if anyone had tried to tell me that at the time,' he said with a twisted grin, 'I wouldn't have believed them. But I can see now that there were a lot of other issues involved as well. Part of the reason why I was so very bitter, was that it came as an enormous blow to my budding ego, to think that I'd come such a long way, but I *still* wasn't good enough for the Fairleighs. Alison was very bitter too because of the way her parents handled the situation. They threatened all sorts of dire consequences for me if we got married and she finally gave in and married Charles Wandsworth because it didn't seem to matter who she married then. But she began to discover that it had been the right choice after all, although it took her some time to come to terms with it.'

Hannah's lips formed a gape of astonishment.

'Yes,' he said and stroked her hair. 'She fell out of love with me and into love with him. When he died like that, it was quite natural that every bit of time she'd wasted agonising over me and what her parents had forced her into, rose up and taunted her.'

Hannah swallowed painfully and brushed the tears from her lashes. 'Oh no,' she said huskily. 'Poor thing—and that's what she meant when she said she'd wasted so much time and you said you were sorry? I thought ... I thought,' her voice was distressed, 'that ...'

'I know,' he said. 'At least I suspected,' he added broodingly.

'How?' she whispered.

'Only thanks to Marge. After you ran away, she told me how you'd come to know of Alison Fairleigh in the first place. Marge insisted that something must have happened to make you think—make you *sure* Alison and I were still in love. Which made me think back very carefully. And I remembered you going to make the coffee that night and taking a long time about it and looking a bit strange when you came back. I remembered what we'd been saying and how, in the light of Marge's news, it could have sounded. It's been that sliver of hope that's stopped me going insane these last few months,' he said very quietly, and trailed his fingers down her neck to let them lie in the hollows at the base of her throat. 'In spite of what Marge also told me—not to believe one word of that letter.'

'But you did ... I mean ...'

'Hannah, sometimes it was hard not to. I'd never known you to lie, for one thing.' He held her close as she was wracked by a shudder of guilt. 'I just couldn't understand why you hadn't told me about the baby, for another thing. So I couldn't help wondering if it was not so much because of thinking I was still in love with Alison, but that it came as a shock to you to find you were pregnant. I mean it's all very well to dream of babies but the reality of them is—can be, to discover that you're trapped . . .'

Hannah moved convulsively. 'It wasn't that. I wanted that baby more than anything I've ever wanted, but I knew you didn't think I was ready for it. Then, when I lost it, it seemed like Fate. As if,' she said, her voice barely audible, 'it was the way out for us all.'

'Why did you think that?' he asked after a moment. 'That I didn't think you were ready for it.'

She told him what she had overheard the night of the lion cub incident. 'Do you remember?' she asked shakily.

'Hannah, my love, that wasn't what I meant . . .'

'I think it was,' she said, with a tremulous little smile. 'You were so angry with me.'

'Yes I was,' he agreed wryly. 'But mainly because I came very close to losing you that day and the thought of that does strange things to me.' He looked at her consideringly and she felt her pulses leap. 'But when I said what I did later, it was for another reason,' he went on. 'Guilt . . . which has plagued me since not very long after I first got to know you. You asked me just now why I hadn't told you how I felt. In fact I did once and you wouldn't believe me.'

'I . . . don't remember that.' Her voice cracked.

'Do you remember coming to me one morning,' something in his voice made her tremble, 'and trying to convince me that we shouldn't get married?'

'Yes, but . . .'

'And do you remember me asking you if you'd believe that I'd fallen in love with you?'

She caught her breath and went quite still.

'And if, my darling,' he smudged the tears on her cheeks with unsteady fingers, 'you'd been a mind reader, you'd have known that as long ago as the time we had a discussion about Billy Johnson, in particular, and men in general, even while I was dispensing such fatherly advice, I was already very much attracted to you myself. Which was an ironic state of affairs, you must admit.'

Her lips parted.

'Mmm,' he agreed. 'I was in a right dilemma, although I have to admit that up until then I thought I was handling things rather well. I'd told myself that you were too young to know about love, that you'd quite possibly be frightened if you knew how I sometimes thought of you; that you needed time, a chance to spread your wings. I even told myself that you needed to learn a bit more about men before you were expected to look into your heart and decide if you were in love—only I discovered that the thought of you learning from anyone else but me, didn't appeal to me in the least,' he said grimly.

'I . . .'

'I know. There was no way you could have known,' he said, 'because I took great care that you didn't— never to know myself,' he said very quietly, 'how I was going to be hoist by my own petard, if you like, and you see, I had other problems too. For years I'd— taken a sort of pride in being a little detached, a little on the outside of my affairs with women. Not because I was still in love with Alison but because I was . . . just wary, I think. While I knew I'd got over her and was happy to think she'd found true love, I couldn't quite forget the trauma of it. When you came into my life, for a while I tried to tell myself it wasn't happening to me. I thought, after all these years and all the women I've known, *can* it be happening to me? I think I'd come to believe it couldn't somehow. But when you came back in the rain that night, and I saw what Matt Bartholomew had done to you, I knew that it had. For several reasons. I could have *killed* him, and I knew that I had to make sure it could never happen again because I just couldn't bear it. Unfortunately, as I think your father always knew, I have a streak of ... I don't know what you'd call it ...'

'An untamed streak?' she whispered, thinking of what Marge had said once.

He smiled slightly. 'Perhaps. Whatever it is, it'll always be there. You see, I wasn't sorry afterwards. I know I should have been, because I'd known since the night I kissed you in the lemon grove, that I was probably kindling some adolescent dreams for you. But I wasn't sorry—not sorry that I'd done it at least. Only sorry that it had had to happen that way, without you knowing how I felt, and not able to believe it.'

'I thought they might be adolescent too,' she said, 'but they've never changed. Alex ...'

'Don't make me feel worse—not that I don't deserve it,' he said wryly.

'No ... I was going to say,' she swallowed painfully, 'I was going to say that I sometimes *felt* too young for you. I felt so shy and gauche. And ... and that night you showed me you could make me want you even when I was angry with you and I thought I hated you—I felt so hopeless, so ...'

'Hannah.' He picked up her hand and held it. 'I took you in anger and a certain amount of despair that night. You see, in lieu of being able to tell you, credibly, how much I loved you, and incidentally, in lieu of putting you on the spot, something I was strangely afraid to do, I decided to show you. As time went by I even thought I was succeeding. Then you changed and I didn't know why. All I could think of was that you *had* been too young and you were realising it and coming to want to spread your wings. That's why I was angry and desperate. But what you hadn't had time to learn, is that sex is the very special way a man and a woman in love express themselves. So it often reflects their tensions and fears as well as love and tenderness. It's not a static thing. You should never feel guilty about it, if it draws a response from you even in anger. We were both angry that night, but we were both deeply moved by each other. That's the important thing.'

'Do you mean, you wouldn't have done it if you hadn't . . . if you hadn't . . .'

'No. If I hadn't had the awful feeling you were slipping away from me, no . . .'

She lay silent in his arms for a long time. Then she said in a shaky voice, 'So you don't mind being my . . . teacher, my friend and my guardian—all those things?'

'I never wanted it any other way, Hannah. And I hope you believe me because if you don't, I'll have to go on trying to make you.'

'Oh, Alex,' she whispered. 'What a fool I've been.'

'No,' he said huskily, 'not you.'

'Yes.' She clung to him and wept into his shoulder. 'Not only that, but to think of what a liar I became! And I used to be so self-righteous about those things!'

'Hannah . . .' he breathed, 'look at me.'

'I don't think I can,' she gulped. 'I feel too burdened down with so many sins. Why?'

'Because I want to kiss you, that's why,' he said and when she lifted her head finally, he smiled down at her with amusement and love and tenderness and a glint of naked desire in his eyes, so that she trembled in his arms. He said, 'If you love me the way I love you, don't you think we could put all our sins behind us now? Your imagined ones and my real ones?'

'Oh . . . if . . . yes, please . . .'

And those were the last words she said for a long time, other than his name, because he kissed her lingeringly. They made love on the settee, in the moonlight and for Hannah it was like a welding together of all the times he had made love to her, a blending of the gentleness, and the expertise that made her body ache with desire and respond as it had once before, but this time lovingly and joyfully.

They lay together for a long time afterwards, with their legs entwined and their arms about each other, not talking, just savouring a closer closeness that was all the more precious because it had been so nearly lost.

Until he said, 'I've got just one thing to ask you.'

'Anything . . .'

He laughed quietly and kissed her. 'Nothing earth-shattering. It's just that the Reverend Clayton verbally consigned me to hell, and meant every word of it. I think my . . . image needs some restoring in his eyes.'

'Oh!' Hannah bit her lip guiltily. 'Oh, I'm so sorry. It will be the first thing I do when I get home. But you know, the only . . . dubious thing, if that's the right word, I ever told him about you, was that I didn't think you loved me really.'

'That would have been enough for him,' Alex said humorously. 'But no, seriously, I can understand how he felt and I find it's important to me to regain his esteem.'

'He'll be so happy,' Hannah said softly. 'Alex, this is like a dream come true. Perhaps I shouldn't say it, but I think I might need to be reminded it is true quite often. Then I won't mind when you get cross with me at having to rescue me from the consequences of my follies and so on.'

He said, 'Until I started rescuing you from the consequences of your follies, as you put it, I didn't know I was alive, sweetheart. Even though I got cross sometimes, I've long since realised that the reason you get into more trouble than most of us, is because you refuse to allow your conscience ever to take the easy way out as so many people do, and that's one of the things I love about you so very much.'

Her eyes shone. 'That's one of the nicest things you've ever said to me. I feel like an equal now. Although . . .'

'Although what, my love?' he asked.

'. . . Perhaps I ought to get it in writing,' she teased.

Here's how to get this special offer from Harlequin!

September
BETTY NEELS
TREASURY EDITION
COUPON

As simple as 1…2…3!

1. Each month, save one Treasury Edition coupon from your favorite Romance or Presents novel.
2. In four months you'll have saved four Treasury Edition coupons (only one coupon per month allowed).
3. Then all you have to do is fill out and return the order form provided, along with the four Treasury Edition coupons required and $2.95 for postage and handling.

Mail to: Harlequin Reader Service

In the U.S.A.
901 Fuhrmann Blvd.
P.O. Box 1397
Buffalo, NY 14240

In Canada
P.O. Box 609
Fort Erie, Ontario
L2A 9Z9

BN-Sep-2

Please send me my Special copy of the Betty Neels Treasury Edition. I have enclosed the four Treasury Edition coupons required and $2.95 for postage and handling along with this order form. (Please Print)

NAME_____

ADDRESS_____

CITY_____

STATE/PROV._____ ZIP/POSTAL CODE_____

SIGNATURE_____

This offer is limited to one order per household.

SUPPLIES LIMITED

This special Betty Neels offer expires
February 28, 1987.